"I'm scared you're going to take Timmy away," Kari said.

"He was taken from me." David couldn't stop himself from reaching out and touching her arm. Her skin was as velvety soft and warm as he remembered.

Immediately she tensed.

It wasn't the reaction he wanted. "Don't be afraid of me, Kari. I'm not going to hurt you."

Looking into his eyes, Kari knew that wasn't true. He could hurt her. He could make her care what happened to him, make her want what she couldn't have. His only interest was his son. She had to remember that....

Dear Reader,

What's a single FABULOUS FATHER to do when he discovers he has another daughter—a child he never knew about? Why, marry the secretive mom, of course! And that's exactly what he proposes in Moyra Tarling's *Twice a Father*. Don't miss this wonderful story.

This month, two authors celebrate the publication of their twenty-fifth Silhouette books! *A Handy Man To Have Around* is Elizabeth August's twenty-fifth book—and part of her bestselling miniseries, SMYTHESHIRE, MASSACHUSETTS. In this delightful novel, a tall, dark and gorgeous hunk sure proves to be A Handy Man To Have Around when a small-town gal needs big-time help!

Daddy on the Run is Carla Cassidy's twenty-fifth book for Silhouette—and part of her intriguing miniseries THE BAKER BROOD. In this heartwarming tale, a married dad can finally come home—to his waiting wife and daughter.

In Toni Collins's *Willfully Wed*, a sexy private investigator learns who anonymously left a lovely lady a potful of money. But telling the truth could break both their hearts!

Denied his child for years, a single dad wants his son—*and* the woman caring for the boy—in *Substitute Mom* by Maris Soule.

And finally, there's only one thing a bachelor cop with a baby on his hands can do: call for maternal backup in Cara Colter's *Baby in Blue*.

Six wonderful love stories by six talented authors—that's what you'll find this and every month in Silhouette Romance!

Enjoy every one...

Melissa Senate
Senior Editor

Please address questions and book requests to:
Silhouette Reader Service
U.S.: 3010 Walden Ave., P.O. Box 1325, Buffalo, NY 14269
Canadian: P.O. Box 609, Fort Erie, Ont. L2A 5X3

SUBSTITUTE MOM

Maris Soule

Silhouette
ROMANCE™
Published by Silhouette Books
America's Publisher of Contemporary Romance

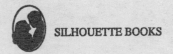

SILHOUETTE BOOKS

ISBN 0-373-19160-X

SUBSTITUTE MOM

This edition published by arrangement with Harlequin Books S.A.

® and TM are trademarks of Harlequin Books S.A., used under license. Trademarks indicated with ® are registered in the United States Patent and Trademark Office, the Canadian Trade Marks Office and in other countries.

Printed in U.S.A.

Books by Maris Soule

Silhouette Romance

Missy's Proposition #864
Lyon's Pride #930
No Strings Attached #965
Stop the Wedding! #1038
Substitute Mom #1160

MARIS SOULE

was born in California but now lives in Michigan with
her husband and family. The author of numerous cate-
gory romances, she is now happy to be writing for the
Silhouette Romance line. Maris believes that marriage
takes a lot of commitment and energy, but it is the best
thing that can happen to a person. When Maris and her
husband married, they decided to take one year at a
time, renewing their "unwritten" contract each May.
So far they've renewed it 28 times—not bad in this
day and age!

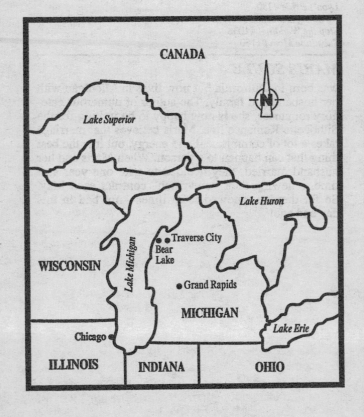

CANADA

Lake Superior

Lake Huron

Lake Michigan

• Traverse City
• Bear
Lake

WISCONSIN

• Grand Rapids

MICHIGAN

Chicago •

Lake Erie

ILLINOIS

INDIANA

OHIO

Prologue

"You're going where?" Kari Carmichael stared at the woman seated across the kitchen table from her.

"Paris." Gail's face was radiant with excitement. "Can you believe it? Paris, France. I've always wanted to go there. Here all I was hoping for when I applied for that job was a decent salary and good benefits. Little did I know one of the benefits would be traveling with the boss." She grinned. "One very handsome, *eligible* boss, I might add. Oh, Kari, this is a chance of a lifetime."

Kari had heard that before. Gail was always looking for that "chance of a lifetime." First when she ran for high school cheerleader. Later when she took off for New York to become a model. Then again when she headed for Los Angeles, certain her chance for happiness lay there.

Not that Gail had had an easy life. She hadn't. And the past few years had been rough ones. Two weeks ago, she'd buried her mother. Three years before that, she'd buried a husband. Here she was, just twenty-eight years old, an orphan, a widow and a single parent. Kari glanced down at the towheaded four-year-old playing near their feet. "What about Timmy?"

"He's why I'm here." Gail looked at her with those soulful blue eyes of hers. "I need your help."

"Help?" Kari asked cautiously.

"Will you watch him?"

Kari was quite sure they were talking about more than just "watching" Timmy, yet she could probably do it for a week.

"It would only be for three months," Gail said. "I'll be back before Christmas."

"Three months!" Kari exclaimed and Timmy looked her way.

"That's how long Vernon, I mean, Mr. Price plans on being in Paris. Please..." Gail stretched out the word. "Timmy won't be any trouble. He loves you, and he'd give you lots of ideas for books. You said yourself you'd like to illustrate something you wrote yourself but can't come up with any ideas your publisher likes. Three months with Timmy, and you'll have tons of ideas."

Kari wasn't convinced. "My home is my studio. This place isn't kid-safe. He could get hurt."

"I'll help you make the place kid-safe."

"I have the illustrations for *Trolls, Fairies and Tommy Magoo* to finish by December."

"You can do them. Televisions are wonderful baby-sitters, and Timmy goes to bed early. You could put him down for naps in the afternoon. Or what about Ralph? Couldn't he watch Timmy once in a while?"

Kari laughed. "Ralph, watch Timmy? I don't think so. Ralph's not exactly wild about kids."

"Well, being around Timmy might *get* Ralphy-boy wild about kids. Then maybe he would pop the question."

"I'm not sure I want 'Ralphy-boy' popping the question."

"Sure you do," Gail insisted. "How long have you two been going out? Eight months? Nine?"

Kari quickly figured back to when she'd bought her computer from Ralph Schneider and he'd installed it in her home. "It's been ten months."

"Ten months," Gail repeated. "One month after David and I met, we were married. Ten months later I gave birth to Timmy. Why waste time, Kari? The guy's perfect for you. Quiet. Steadfast. Financially sound."

"Oh, great. Now you sound like my father."

Gail knew how her father's preoccupation with financial security irked Kari, and she quickly changed the subject. "Okay, forget Ralph. Do this for me. Please—"

"I don't know."

"Come on." Again Gail gave her a wistful look. "Feel sorry for me. I haven't had all the breaks you have, and these past few years have been hell. Losing David, now Mom..." She sighed dramatically. "Sure I could forget this job, take something else, but where would it get me? I don't want to end up like my mother."

"You're not going to end up like your mother."

"Think of all I've done for you. You never would have gotten to go to the Chicago Institute of Art if I hadn't convinced your father you would be miserable in the business world and had a God-given art talent. And you wouldn't be illustrating children's books and have that Caldecott Award if I hadn't taken your portfolio around to all those New York publishing houses."

"If you hadn't *stolen* my portfolio and taken it around," Kari reminded her.

Gail grinned. "So are you complaining?"

"No." She could never thank her friend enough. "All right. You win. I'll do it. I'll watch Timmy while you go to Paris." Kari laughed. "For your 'chance of a lifetime.'"

Chapter One

Within a week, Kari regretted her decision. A four-year-old, she discovered, was constant motion, constant noise and constant curiosity. Everything had to be explained, and not once, but over and over.

It wouldn't be so bad, she told herself, if Timmy were sweet and loving, but he seemed to blame her for his mother's absence. Over and over, Kari explained to him why Gail had gone to Paris. It didn't stop the door slamming, the throwing of things or the swearing. "I'm going to end up with a book, all right," she mumbled after putting him down for an afternoon nap. "It's going to be titled, *Timmy's Angry.*"

Before she began that book, however, she needed to finish the paintings for the troll book. Certain all was quiet behind Timmy's closed door, Kari went to her studio. The pencil sketches had been approved with the editor suggesting only minor changes, and she'd begun the final work.

Kari sat down at her art table and picked up a 2H pencil. Her love of Persian art was evident in all of her work, each painting a complex design of gemlike parts. The drawing in front of her was no exception. The watercolor paper was covered with trolls and fairies, mushrooms and ferns, butterflies and moths. Hidden among them all was the little boy Tommy Magoo. Only a few more details and it would be time to put on the first wash of color.

She added more cross-hatching to the troll under the bridge, then paused, letting her thoughts drift back to Timmy. The boy wasn't really bad, just angry. His father had deserted him by dying. His grandmother had just done the same. And now his mother was gone, and he'd been left with someone he barely knew.

In the same situation, she would probably slam things, or throw them or swear.

Not that she could allow him to continue with that behavior. She'd had to set ground rules and had had to discipline him. Not that she was all that certain sending him to his room was a good form of punishment. The boy was alone too much of the time as it was. He needed children to play with, and next time she talked to Gail, she was going to suggest enrolling Timmy in a nursery school.

A knock on her front door startled her out of her thoughts. Putting down her pencil, she slid off her stool and headed for the door. It could be Ralph. He'd said he had a computer program that would knock her socks off and make the graphic designs she did for the local merchants as easy as one-two-three. It had sounded good to her.

She opened her door wide, a welcoming smile on her face. Then she gasped.

The day was warm for mid-September, but a chill ran down Kari's spine. Past and present slammed into each other, confusion reigning. Dumbfounded, she stared at the man standing on her stoop, her mouth open but no words coming out.

He stood with his arms folded across his chest, his lips pressed together, and his blue eyes narrowed in a scowl. A stubble of blond beard covered his cheeks and chin, and if anything had combed through his hair lately, it had been his fingers. From the limp, wrinkled look of his white cotton shirt and tan khakis, Kari doubted he'd changed clothes recently. Pale and haggard, he looked like death warmed over, which seemed most appropriate.

The man standing in front of her was supposed to be dead.

"Where is he?" he demanded, his voice menacingly harsh.

Still too stunned to think straight, Kari asked, "Who?"

His glare intensified. "My son. Timmy. He's here, isn't he? That's what the woman I talked to said. She said Gail was in Paris and you had my son."

"I, ah..." Frantically, Kari tried to pull herself together. What was happening couldn't be. This had to be a dream, a nightmare. "Timmy's father is dead."

"Do I look dead?"

Though she'd only seen pictures of him, he looked dead tired, rumpled and churlish, but otherwise very much alive. It didn't make sense. "Gail said you died in a car accident."

"Sounds like a story she'd come up with." He pulled his wallet from his back pocket and flipped it open, showing his California driver's license. "Read what it says. I'm David Weeks, Timmy's father, and I'm very much alive. Now give me my son."

What his license said was David Weeks was thirty-two, had blond hair and blue eyes, was five feet eleven inches in height and weighed one hundred eighty pounds. The statistics checked out, and the picture wasn't bad for a driver's license, but it didn't capture the animal magnetism of the man standing in front of her, the coiled power she sensed, or the man's anger.

It also didn't explain anything. "But the accident?"

"There was no accident. Now, are you going to get my son for me or do I have to get him myself?"

The possibility of his taking Timmy stirred Kari into action. Boldly, she spread her arms, resting her hands on each side of the doorway and forming a human blockade. "Timmy was left in my care. I am not giving him to anyone, no matter who you say you are."

"And I didn't just spend the past two and a half days driving cross-country to argue with you."

He pushed her aside as if she were no more than a turnstile, and entered her house. Moving without even thinking, Kari grabbed his arm and set her feet, bracing herself for a fight. "Timmy's taking a nap and is not to be disturbed."

Beneath her fingertips, his muscles tensed. He looked down at her, the blue of his eyes pure ice, and for a moment she thought he was going to shove her aside. Then he took in a deep breath, and his expression softened. "Gail told me about you."

Kari didn't relax. "She told me about you, too."

And had sent her pictures.

David had been another of Gail's "chances of a lifetime," and for once in all the years she'd known Gail, Kari had envied her. David Weeks had looked more like a sexy movie star than an accountant, and everything Gail had written about him had sounded too good to be true. Were there really men out there who didn't lie? Who listened to what a woman said and understood? Or who were as loving and sexy as Gail had described David?

Kari wasn't sure if the man standing in front of her was telling the truth or if he was listening to her, but he sure looked sexy, in a rugged, disheveled way. Okay, yes, he definitely had sex appeal. Too much sex appeal, she decided, gazing into his eyes. Quickly, she looked down at the floor.

He made a derisive sound. "I'm surprised you actually exist."

Again, she looked up. "Well, I do. And Gail left Timmy in my care, so this is where he's staying until she tells me otherwise. Does *she* know you're alive?"

"Oh, yes." He stared down at her. "Gail actually told you I was dead?"

"She said you were in a car accident. A head-on crash. She said you were killed instantly."

"What a liar. Everything. Every damned word out of that woman's mouth is a lie."

David took a closer look at the woman in front of him. Even his ex-wife's description of her best friend had been a lie. Kari Carmichael was small, yes—the top of her head barely made it to his chin—but she was no shy, shrinking violet afraid to say boo to a mouse. And she wasn't plain, as Gail had implied. Not with those big, expressive brown eyes, the high cheekbones and a mouth that looked all too tempting. No, the woman keeping him from his son was spunky, pretty and downright desirable. That, or he'd simply been isolated from women too long.

"Gail tends to exaggerate," Kari defended.

"I wouldn't call saying she'd been born and raised in New York City an exaggeration," he argued. "Or telling you I was dead. I've spent the past three months trying to track her down. You know why? Because nothing she'd told me was the truth. Not about her family, her childhood or anything. Her 'exaggerations' are so numerous, I had to hire a private detective. If it hadn't been for him, I doubt I ever would have found out she'd been born and raised in northern Michigan, or that she had a mother living here in Bear Lake."

"Who just recently died," Kari said. "You've got to understand Gail. She's always been embarrassed by her background. From the time she was a little girl, she's wanted to escape her life here, be someone different. She only came back this time because there was no one to take care of her mother."

"So what's she escaping now? Timmy? Is that why she took off for Paris and dumped my son on you?"

"No," Kari argued. "She's not escaping anything. She had to get a job, she had no money left, and the job she got requires she travel with her boss."

"Three months in Paris with her boss," David repeated, doubting the arrangement was as innocent as stated. Either Kari Carmichael was as big a liar as Gail or very naive.

"Yes." Kari nodded and her hair bobbed up and down in a silken cascade of mahogany over her shoulders, drawing his gaze lower. He liked the way her white T-shirt, with its butterfly design, accentuated the rounded curves of her breasts. He liked the way her denim cutoffs hugged her hips and showed off her tanned legs. He even liked the shape of her feet, pink polish highlighting her toenails.

A tightening in his loins surprised him, and he brought his gaze back to her face. This was no time for long-deprived hormones to kick in. He was here for one thing only. "Look, it doesn't really matter what Gail told you or where she is now. She wasn't to leave California with Timmy, not without permission, and I've come to get him and to take him back."

"Well, you're not getting him," Kari said firmly, tightening her hold on his arm. "And you're not taking him anywhere."

Her determination was beginning to irk him, and he pulled his arm free. "Look, we're talking about *my* son, not yours."

She moved in front of him, her back straight and her chin high. "Timmy is Gail's child, too."

"She had no right to take him out of California, not without letting me know. She was legally bound by that restriction."

"But she thought you were dead."

He shook his head. "You don't get it, do you? She knew I wasn't dead. That was just another of her lies. I no longer fit the image she wanted, so she buried me. Only I'm not staying buried, and I'm not relinquishing my claim on my son."

He was tired of arguing. All he wanted was Timmy. It had been so long since he'd seen him, held him. Three years. Three rotten, miserable years. Would he even recognize his son?

David put his hands on her shoulders to ease her aside and was shocked by how delicate she felt and how tenaciously she resisted his pressure. "I can't let you take him," she said.

"He's my son," he repeated.

"And he's my responsibility."

The next move, he knew, was his. He could easily overpower her. If she weighed more than a hundred pounds, he'd be surprised. She'd be no match for his strength. But what then? Tie her up while he got Timmy? Lock her in a room? That was all he'd need, to be arrested for assault and battery. Besides, he'd never rough-handled a woman before, and he wasn't about to begin now.

"You drove from California in two and a half days?"

Her question caught him off guard. For a second he said nothing, then nodded. "Made it in fifty-six hours."

"Have you had any sleep?"

He shrugged. "A little."

"Very little, I'd say." Her look softened and so did her voice. "You look tired."

"I am," he admitted, suddenly aware of how tired he was. His back and shoulders ached, and his eyes felt as though they'd been blasted with sand.

"There are several motels around here, and it's the end of the summer tourist season, so I know you wouldn't have any trouble finding a room. Why don't you get some sleep, clean up a little, then come back. Timmy will be awake then, and you'd feel better."

David hated to admit it, but what she was saying made sense. He *was* tired. If he did go in and get Timmy, what would he do after that? Keep driving?

As tempting as the thought was, it wouldn't be safe. The past two hours on the highway, he'd barely been able to keep his lids open. He didn't need to find his son, then kill him in an accident. His best bet was to do as Kari was suggesting—find a room, get some sleep, then come back for Timmy. "You might be right," he admitted.

Internally , Kari sighed in relief. For a moment she'd thought he was actually going to push her aside and take Timmy, and she hadn't known what to do. Changing the subject had been the only thing she could think of. Now if she could just get him out of her house.

"Bear's Lair is a nice motel," she said. "It's just down the road a way. Betty's the owner. Betty Hoffstein. Tell her I sent you and to give you a good deal."

"Bear's Lair," he repeated, nodding. He rubbed a hand over his chin, then glanced down at his rumpled clothing. "I must look a mess."

"You look like a man who's been on the road too many hours. Get some sleep, then we can talk, and you can explain how you've come back from the dead."

"Right." He laughed sarcastically.

He turned and started for the door, but before he reached it, he stopped and looked back. "He's all right?"

"Timmy?" she asked.

David nodded.

"He's fine." She realized something. "He looks like you. Not only the blond hair and blue eyes, but he's got your smile." Not that she'd seen David Weeks smile all that much, but when he did, it was a smile that made her feel warm all over. "Timmy's really a smart kid. Energetic. Curious."

"He was, even as a baby."

She was touched by the look of pride on his face. Under other circumstances, she would have welcomed his arrival, but there were too many unanswered questions surrounding David Weeks. All she wanted now was to get him out of her house. "Don't forget to tell Betty at Bear's Lair that I sent you."

"I'll do that," he agreed and continued toward the door.

He paused before he stepped outside and looked back. "You say his hair's still blond?"

"Lighter than yours," she answered, willing him to take the next step—out of her home and out of her life. "Almost white."

"Could I just look at him?"

He took a step, but it was back inside, and her stomach did a twist. "It would be better if you didn't. Think of Timmy," she said, hoping she didn't sound as desperate as she felt. "He really needs his sleep, and if we go in there, we're liable to wake him. He hasn't seen you for three years. He thinks you're dead. I don't know how he's going to react. You don't know how he's going to react, and you're tired."

David glanced around her small house, first at the closed door to her bedroom, then toward her studio. Frowning, he looked back at her. "And when I come back, will you have taken off with Timmy?"

"Why should I?" she asked. "If you're Timmy's father, then he should be with you." Except, she was sure something wasn't on the up-and-up, and she intended to find out what it was. "Timmy and I will be here," she promised. He was the one who wouldn't be back, not if she was right.

She didn't let out her breath until the door actually clicked closed behind him. Then she hurried over and bolted the lock, something she'd never done before in the four years she'd lived in the house. Watching out the window, she saw him walk to his car, get in and back up. As soon as the vehicle pulled onto the road and headed toward town and the Bear's Lair motel, Kari hurried into her kitchen and the telephone.

Her hand shaking, she grabbed the phone book. Calling 9-1-1 would bring the emergency vehicles; she wanted just the law. She found the number for the sheriff's department and punched it in. *Be calm,* she told herself, her heart beating faster than a hummingbird's. *Everything's going to be all right.*

She thought she made herself perfectly clear the first time she explained the situation to the deputy who answered, but when she had to explain what had happened a second time and then a third, she began to wonder if the man understood English. "David Weeks is supposed to be dead," she said again. "But he's here, or was here. He has a driver's license that says he's who he says he is, and he looks like the pictures Gail sent me, but I have no way of knowing who he really is . . . and he wants Timmy."

By the time she'd again explained who Timmy was and why he was at her house and where Gail was and why, Kari was about ready to scream. "All I want you to do is arrest this man. You should find him at the Bear's Lair motel—that's where I sent him. Or if not there, at some motel. He was tired. Dead tired. And he's driving a cream-colored Chevy.

"No, I don't know what model," she answered when the deputy asked. "And no, I didn't get the license number." She chided herself for not doing that. "I just know something's not right, and I want you to keep him away from here."

Her entire body was shaking by the time she hung up. The officer had at least promised to look into the matter. She'd hoped for more assurance, a guarantee that she wouldn't have to face David Weeks again.

How could he be alive if Gail had said he was dead?

That question kept running though her head as she searched for the note Gail had given her when she'd dropped off Timmy's things. On it, Kari knew, was the name of the hotel where Gail was staying.

She found the note pinned to the bulletin board in her studio, exactly where she'd put it. Using the phone in there, she punched in the numbers and waited. She'd taken a year of French when she was in college, mostly because so many painters she was studying were French, but she'd barely managed a C grade and had forgotten most of what she'd learned. She did recognize *"Bonsoir,"* when the man on the other end of the line answered. Haltingly, she tried to come up with the words that would get her Gail's room. Kari sighed in relief when the man switched to English and connected her.

With the time difference, Kari expected Gail to be in, but after the eighth ring, the man at the desk came back on the line. She had to be satisfied with leaving a message for Gail to call as soon as possible. Hanging up, Kari sagged down on her stool and stared out her studio window.

She could see Bear Lake in the distance, the water a crystal blue. And she could see the rooftops of the homes and businesses that made up the small resort town of Bear Lake. Somewhere down there a cream-colored Chevy was pulling into a motel and a man was getting out.

Over and over, she asked herself, *Can it really have been David Weeks?*

Chapter Two

Kari's telephone rang at six-thirty that night. Dinner was over and she was cleaning the kitchen while Timmy played in the living room. The moment she heard Gail's voice, Kari sighed in relief. "Boy, am I glad to hear from you. Where have you been? I called and left a message hours ago."

"I've, ah...been, ah...at a meeting," Gail answered. "I just got back to my room and got your message. What's up?"

A quick glance into the living room confirmed that Timmy was busy playing with his stuffed dinosaur; nevertheless, Kari lowered her voice. "A man came by the house this afternoon. He says he's David...David Weeks, that he didn't die in a car accident, that you lied about that. He also said you weren't supposed to take Timmy out of California, and that you—"

"David is in Michigan?"

"I know it's impossible—"

"He's out of jail?"

"Jail?" Kari swallowed hard, letting the word sink in.

"Oh, God." Gail sighed the words. "They must have given him time off for good behavior."

"Your husband was in jail? He didn't die in a car accident?" Kari was completely confused.

"Damn!" Gail swore. "He's going to screw up everything."

"But you said..." Kari was still trying to make sense of what was happening.

"What did you expect me to say?" Gail snapped. "That my husband was a crook?"

"No, but—"

"I don't believe this."

"He was right here." Kari remembered the way David had looked and acted when she first opened her door. "And he was really upset. I thought he was going to forcibly take Timmy."

"He took Timmy?"

"No. I talked him out of it."

"Thank goodness for that. How in the hell did he find out where Timmy was?"

"I guess your neighbor told him. He knew that you're in Paris and that I had Timmy."

"No, I mean, how'd he track me to Michigan?"

"He said he hired a detective. He said you lied about your past."

"Lies. Fibs. You know me, Kari. I like to stretch the truth a bit." Gail passed it off as nothing. "How'd you get rid of him?"

"He looked really tired. I talked him into getting a room at Bear's Lair and getting some sleep. I told him we could talk later. Then, after he left, I called the sheriff's department."

"Good for you. And what did the sheriff have to say?"

"The deputy I talked to said he'd look into it. I really didn't think it was David. I mean, he looked like the pictures you'd sent, and he had a driver's license, but since you'd said he was dead, I—"

"Is he still as good-looking?" Gail interrupted.

"Yes. I mean, I guess." Kari wasn't sure what she was comparing him to. She'd only seen the pictures Gail had sent. "He was really tired. He said he'd driven two and a half days straight. And—"

Again, Gail interrupted. "I wonder if he escaped from prison. I know they're always paroling people before their time's up, but this soon?"

"Escaped?" Kari tried to remember how David had acted when he was with her. Had he been furtive? Wary?

"Well, don't worry." Gail laughed. "If he did, he'll undoubtedly screw that up, too."

"What did he screw up before? What did he do?"

"Embezzled money. Lots and lots of money. Money I thought was ours. After they arrested him, I couldn't touch a cent. Not one damn cent."

David Weeks was an embezzler. Kari decided that was better than being a robber who walked into a store or bank and pointed a gun at the cashier. And it was definitely better than being a murderer. Still, a shiver ran down her spine. "You've got to come back. Right away."

A knock on her front door caught her attention. Timmy cried out, "I'll get it."

"No!" she yelled to him, but too late. Timmy had already thrown the bolt and was opening the door.

Kari prayed it would be Ralph. Or a neighbor or a friend. Even the sheriff's deputy would be a welcome sight.

Her heart dropped to her toes when she saw the man standing on her stoop, and she let out a groan.

"What's the matter?" Gail asked.

"It's David."

Kari watched him step into her house and scoop up Timmy. The boy wiggled in his arms, turning toward her, a panicky look in his eyes. "Put him down!" she yelled, moving as far into the living room as her telephone cord permitted.

David looked her way, a frown immediately creasing his brow. Timmy continued to wiggle in his arms, whining and kicking.

"Call 9-1-1," Gail ordered over the phone.

"Get back here right away," Kari cried into the phone, then hit the disconnect button and quickly dialed 9-1-1.

Just as quickly, David set Timmy back down on the carpeting. Four long strides took him across the living room. He grabbed the telephone from her hand and pressed the disconnect button, then dropped the phone to the floor. Kari bent to retrieve it, only to feel large hands wrapping around her waist. Lifted off her feet, she wiggled, but couldn't stop him from turning her in his arms and setting her down so she was facing him. The instant he released his hold, she bolted, only to be grabbed again. Holding on to her T-shirt, he pulled her tight against his body.

"What the hell do you think you're doing?" he demanded, his breath hot on her cheek.

"Nothing," she said, unable to move. Her left arm was caught between them, intimately resting across his crotch, her hand twisted so it was of no use. With her breasts squashed into his chest, every beat of his heart reverberated through her, every breath he took intensifying the contact.

"Who were you calling?"

"I was talking to Gail," she snapped.

"I mean after you hung up."

"Let her go," Timmy demanded from near their feet, his little voice quavering.

He stood with his fists clenched and his feet wide apart. David moved slightly to glance down at the boy, the motion intensifying the contact against her breasts. "I'm not going to hurt her," he told Timmy.

"You're a bad man. Go away!" Timmy yelled.

"I'm your father."

"No, you're not. No, you're not." With each word, Timmy's voice grew louder. Nevertheless, Kari could hear another sound. The phone lay on the floor by his feet, its cord stretching to the kitchen. Disconnected, it had begun to beep.

"I told Gail you were here," Kari said. "She's coming back."

"Glad to hear it. Too bad Timmy and I will miss her."

"You can't take him." She struggled to get loose, but only succeeded in twisting herself into a more intimate position.

"Let her go!" Timmy yelled.

Kari tried to think, but with her hand pressed against a very male part of David's anatomy and Timmy screaming hysterically, that wasn't easy to do. *Stay calm,* she told herself. *Use logic.*

The logic was, if she didn't do something, by tomorrow David would be long gone with Timmy. After that...

She'd read about incidents where fathers kidnapped their children, taking them away from their mothers, never to be seen again. She had to do something, say something to convince David to stay. Or at least to get him to release his bearlike hold on her. Then she had to get help.

She forced herself to sound nonthreatening. "Why leave? Wouldn't it be better to stay so you and Gail could talk this out, iron out whatever problems you've had."

"Talk?" He laughed. "About what? Loyalty? Honesty? What she'll do is tell me lies, then disappear with my son."

"No, Gail wouldn't do that," Kari insisted. "What she did before... Well, she explained that to me on the phone. She was embarrassed. And the reason she didn't tell you she was taking Timmy out of the state was because you were in jail and her mother needed her immediately. She just didn't have time, but I'm sure Gail was going to let you know where she was, where Timmy was.''

"When, Kari? She's been here six months. When was she going to tell me? In a year? When Timmy was grown?''

"I don't know.'' The fact that Gail had been in Michigan for more than six months and hadn't contacted David didn't bode well.

"I think you do know. I think you're helping her.''

"No,'' Kari insisted.

"Aren't you?'' He glowered down at her, tightening his hold, and Kari closed her eyes. This was too close to be to a man you were afraid of. Too close to be to a man who made your blood rush.

"I didn't contest the divorce, you know,'' he said. "But it wasn't my idea. When I made those wedding vows, I intended to stick to them—through sickness and health, for better or for worse. And if things had been reversed, I would have stuck by her, been willing to wait. I didn't want a divorce. Nevertheless, I tried to see things from her point of view, tried to understand.

"Nor did I contest her having custody of Timmy. How could I? I certainly couldn't take care of him, not from behind bars. And I didn't argue when she said she didn't want to bring him to see me. She was right, having him see his father in prison would not have been good for him. But damn it all, she wasn't to take him out of the state.''

"Her mother was dying,'' Kari argued, wishing he would understand.

"The mother she was too ashamed to tell me about? The mother she never called?'' He scoffed. "What made her so loyal now?''

"You've got to understand Gail,'' Kari argued. "She and her mother never got along well. That she came back at all says a lot for Gail.''

"Damn!'' David yelled and Kari felt him jerk his leg. "He bit me.''

She heard Timmy start crying and looked his way. The boy was huddled on the floor near the phone.

"Now you're kicking your son?"

"I didn't kick him," David argued. "I shook him and his mouth off my leg."

"Does it make you feel big to hold a woman half your size captive and kick your son?"

"I didn't kick him," he repeated and grumbled.

Big wasn't how she was making him feel, though holding Kari so close was having a physical effect on him that he didn't want. It wouldn't be so bad if she'd stand perfectly still, but every time she moved her hand—

He gritted his teeth. It also didn't help that she smelled so delectably feminine. It didn't take much to arouse a man who'd been without a woman for more than three years.

Not that he would give in to his needs.

"If I let you go," he asked, "will you promise not to try anything?"

She made no promises. Saying nothing, she glared at him. Not knowing what else to do, he relaxed his hold. Immediately, she stepped back, flexing the arm that had been pinned between them. Then she knelt next to Timmy, gathering him into her arms and cuddling him close.

"He's not my daddy, Aunt Kari," Timmy said with firm conviction. "My daddy's gone to heaven. Mommy said so."

The words tore at David's heart. His own son thought he was dead. He should be the one consoling his child instead, he was the bad guy.

The reality of that fact angered him.

"She didn't have to say I was dead. She could have told him I was away... told him about me."

Without releasing her hold on the boy, Kari looked up at him. "And what should she have said?"

"That I made a mistake and was paying for it." He shook his head and momentarily closed his eyes. "That I was too naive and trusting."

"And did you pay?"

"More than I should have."

Something was different, but he wasn't sure what. She was still crouched on the floor, Timmy on her lap. She was still cuddling the boy close, and was still looking up at him as if he would suddenly swoop down and devour both of them. And then he heard and understood. The phone had stopped beeping its incessant beep.

He did bend down. Picking up the phone, he listened and knew he'd run out of time.

Once again, he pushed the disconnect button. This time he tossed the phone into the kitchen, the handset clunking against the side of a cupboard. "Very smart," he growled, grabbing both her hand and Timmy's and dragging them over to the couch.

Timmy cringed and began crying again, but Kari went with him, a fiery flare in her eyes and a smile on her lips. She'd won, and she knew it, and it galled him that he'd once again been too naive and trusting.

"Feeling pretty proud of yourself, aren't you?" he said, settling her on one side of him on the couch and trying to hold Timmy on his lap.

The boy hit at him, a fist catching David near the eye.

"You're a tiger," David grumbled and wrapped an arm around Timmy, immobilizing him. "You've got quite a punch there, son."

"I'm not your son," Timmy yelled and started kicking.

David let go of Kari's arm and grabbed Timmy's feet, but the moment he released her arm, he knew he'd made another mistake. She was on her feet in a second, and from a side table grabbed a brass lamp, raising it above her head like a club.

"Let him go!" she demanded.

Of the two, he decided, she could inflict the most damage. He let Timmy go, swinging the boy off his lap and safely to the side. In his next motion, he rose to his feet, using his left arm to deflect her blow with the lamp and grabbing for her with his right.

Two and a half years in prison had produced one positive result. Hours of boredom had been eased with workouts in the gym. Physically he was in the best shape he'd ever been in, and overpowering Kari was no problem. He disarmed her of her lamp, the lamp crashing to the floor and the bulb shattering.

"Damn you!" she cursed, glaring up at him.

"No, damn you." He took in a deep breath, trying to calm the adrenaline. "Why do you have to fight me?"

Crouched on the floor, Timmy was crying. Kari tried not to cry, but she couldn't stop the tears. Once again she was at David's mercy, held against her will. The position he was holding her in was too intimate, the situation too frightening. He was hard muscle and volatile anger. Outraged wrath and pure male virility.

"Don't cry," he said softly, and she shuddered.

No man should have a voice as soothing and seductive as his. She needed to hold on to her fear, to ignore the vibrations racing through her.

"I'm not going to hurt you," he said and eased his hold, allowing space between them.

Kari drew back, disturbed by her reactions to being held by him. "Go away," she pleaded, closing her eyes and wishing she could wake up and find it had all been a dream. "Just go away."

"I will." He released a deep breath. "Just as soon as you help me pack my son's clothes."

She snapped her eyes open. "No. You can't take him."

"I not only can, I'm going to."

"Look at him. He's scared to death of you."

They both looked at Timmy. The boy remained crouched in the fetal position on the floor where David had set him, his thumb in his mouth and his eyes wide with fear. Tears slid down his cheeks in silent retribution.

"He wouldn't be afraid of me if it weren't for you." David looked back at her. "And he'll get over it once he gets used to me."

"Gail has custody of him, not you."

"And where is Gail?"

She didn't have to answer. Sirens and flashing lights answered for her. Through her living room window, she could see the sheriff's patrol car, the fire engine and the ambulance.

She felt David tense, then heard his sigh of resignation. It was his smile that surprised her. "Happy now?"

Relieved was a better word. "Go let the sheriff in," she told Timmy.

Timmy hesitated only a moment, then ran to the door. David released his hold on her just before Timmy opened the door. Immediately Kari stepped back. She needed distance between them, a lot of distance. The reactions she'd experienced were too bizarre.

"Did someone from this number call 9-1-1?" asked a middle-aged deputy with a slight potbelly, stepping into the living room, a second, younger and thinner deputy close behind.

The middle-aged deputy looked down at Timmy, who stood fascinated by the flashing lights, then across the room to where David and she stood. Kari noticed both deputies had their hands poised near their holsters. The cavalry had arrived.

"He's a convict," she said, stepping back farther and pointing a finger at David. "Either he's escaped from prison or he's broken his parole. He came here to kidnap his son."

She was amazed by how fast both guns came out. The middle-aged deputy held his on David while the younger deputy walked over and handcuffed him. Timmy watched it all with wide-eyed awe, not even noticing when she lifted him into her arms.

David didn't resist. He just kept looking at her.

She might have been afraid if she'd seen anger in his eyes, or even fear. What she read in his look was disappointment, and it tore at her insides.

"What happened?" the middle-aged deputy asked.

Looking away from David, she explained the situation as concisely as she could. She tried to block out the younger deputy's voice as the man read David his rights. She couldn't ignore the fact that David said nothing, not one word to either of the deputies.

"So this is the same man, the one you called our office about earlier today?" The middle-aged deputy made a note in a small book he took from his pocket.

"The one you people did nothing about," she pointed out.

"We don't go around arresting people just because someone thinks something's wrong," the middle-aged deputy said defensively. "We're running a check on him. Nothing had come back when we were informed of your call."

"I wasn't sure I got through."

The sheriff closed his book and put it back in his pocket. Smiling at Timmy, he patted the boy on the arm. "The dispatch operator thought the caller might be a child dialing the number then hanging up. In cases where someone calls 9-1-1 then hangs up, there's a record of the number and she normally calls back to check if it's truly an emergency. Since your line was disconnected, she figured she'd better get us out here. Jim and I were the closest unit."

"Well, I'm glad you showed up." She glanced back toward David. The deputy named Jim was bringing him toward them, none too gently.

"You shouldn't have come here," she said to David, wishing he never had.

He looked at Timmy. "He's my son."

Kari watched them take him away. Inside her throat was a knot, making swallowing impossible, and tears filled her eyes. He could have said so many things, but none would have torn at her insides like those three simple words.

"It's okay, he's gone now," Timmy reassured her, patting her shoulder.

She looked at the boy and felt a tear slide down her cheek. Then she began laughing. The situation was so ridiculous she couldn't help herself. Here she was crying because she was sad that they'd taken him away. And she was crying because she was glad they'd taken him away. She was relieved and upset, drained and agitated, all at once.

"He won't come back, will he?" Timmy asked, clearly concerned.

"No, he won't come back." They would take him off to prison, and she would never see him again.

Timmy would never see him again.

It didn't seem right.

"He's not really a bad man." She had to explain that. "He just made a mistake."

"Mommy said he was in heaven."

"Your mommy told you that because she didn't want you to know your daddy had made a mistake."

"Mommy said Grandma made lots of mistakes. If I make a mistake, will she send me to heaven?"

"Oh, no...no, no." Kari closed the door and set Timmy down. Explaining things to a child could be tricky. She couldn't tell Timmy the biggest mistake his grandmother had made was smoking two packs of cigarettes a day.

"Your grandmother went to heaven because God needed her there. And your mommy didn't send your daddy to heaven, she just said that because ... Well ..." Kari raised her hands in defeat. "I guess I don't know why she said that. She just did. Shall we hang up the phone and clean up that broken lamp?"

"I'll get the phone," Timmy said, running ahead and scooping it up from the kitchen floor.

Kari sighed and wiped the tears from her eyes. She wished she could wipe the image of David as he walked out the door from her mind.

Chapter Three

Kari called Gail back as soon as she could. She wanted to tell her everything that had happened. She knew she'd be happier when Gail was back in Michigan. Watching a four-year-old was turning into a far more nerve-racking experience than she'd expected.

When the hotel desk clerk intervened after the phone had rung several times in Gail's room and said, "Mademoiselle Weeks is evidently not in," Kari refused to believe him.

"She's got to be in," she insisted. "I just talked to her a little while ago. You must have rung the wrong room."

Two more tries proved futile, and Kari gave up and left a message. She was certain there was a mix-up. Gail wouldn't go out. It was after midnight in Paris. Gail knew her son was in jeopardy. She should have been sitting by the phone, nervously waiting for a call back.

Gail didn't call that night, and Kari tried again in the morning. And again Gail didn't answer.

Certain the hotel clerk was ringing the wrong room, Kari insisted on talking to the manager. By the time she'd hung up, she'd been informed that the hotel had not made a mistake, that the right room had been rung, and that the message she'd left earlier had been picked up. When Kari asked why Gail hadn't called her back, she was curtly apprised that it was not the hotel's responsibility to monitor the activities of its guests.

Ralph called while she was fixing Timmy's breakfast. He'd just heard that emergency vehicles had been at her house the night before and had called immediately to see if she was all right.

Kari appreciated his concern, but she didn't want to talk about it with Timmy around. "It was nothing," she said. "I'll explain later."

"But you're okay?" he asked.

"I'm fine," she lied. "It involved Timmy."

"I told you taking on a four-year-old would mean problems," he said.

She doubted he'd envisioned the problems she was having.

It was her mother, who called from Arizona, who gave Kari hope. "Gail may not have been in her hotel room because she's on her way back to the States," she said.

"Then why didn't the desk clerk say she'd checked out?"

Her mother had an answer. "Gail was probably so upset and busy making the necessary arrangements, she forgot to check out. That or she asked her boss to do it for her. After all, I'm sure he got the room for her."

"She could have called me." Should have, Kari felt.

"Maybe she was so distracted, she didn't think of it."

Kari was not convinced.

After talking to her mother, Kari decided to call the sheriff's department to thank them for their help. Timmy was in the backyard playing, and Kari could easily watch him from the kitchen window.

It took the deputy who answered the phone a minute to check on the case. Kari was then switched to another deputy. His response wasn't what she wanted to hear.

"You let him go?" she repeated.

"Unless you want to come down and press charges," he said, "we have nothing to hold him on."

"Nothing to hold him on? The man's a crook. He was in jail. He may have broken out of jail. At the very least, he must have broken his parole."

She could almost see the man shake his head at every statement she made, and she felt her stomach twist with each answer he gave. "According to the information we received," he said, "David Weeks was accused, tried and imprisoned for embezzlement. He served two years and six months of a ten-year sentence."

"And—?" It was the rest that was important.

"Four months ago, his sentence was reversed. Evidently another man they'd been looking for was arrested in Florida, and as soon as he was in custody, a witness came forth who cleared Weeks."

"So David isn't an embezzler?"

"Not according to what we received from California. David Weeks was cleared of all charges."

Which meant he was free to go where he wanted, including Michigan. "What about his rights to Timmy?"

"I'm not sure about those, ma'am," the deputy said. "He'll have to check on the custody laws here in Michigan. Did sound like he might have a case if his ex did as he said. Taking that boy out of California without clearing it with the courts could, allegedly, be construed as kidnapping."

"You're saying Gail kidnapped her son by bringing him back here?" Kari didn't believe it. "Her own son, whom she has custody of?"

"I said allegedly," the deputy repeated.

"Her mother was dying."

"I'm sure the courts would take that into consideration. You might suggest she see a lawyer."

"This is absurd." Kari watched Timmy chase after a butterfly. Dealing with the law seemed as futile, and a surge of panic was building within her. "Where's David now?"

"I don't know, ma'am."

She couldn't let David take Timmy. "You say I could press charges?"

"Yes. If he assaulted or threatened you in any way, you have a right to press charges."

David Weeks had grabbed her and held her, scared her and threatened her sensibilities; yet had he assaulted her? Did she have a right to press charges?

Kari knew the truth. Not once had David exerted more force than necessary to stop her from calling for help or causing him physical harm. It was her emotions he'd threatened.

He'd held her close to his body, and had made her aware of him as a man. He'd aroused feelings she shouldn't have felt. Worst of all, he'd left her feeling guilty. The look he'd given her when the deputy sheriffs took him away had bothered her all night. In the blue depths of his eyes, she'd seen his pain.

She'd won their battle. She'd kept him from taking his son, the son he hadn't seen for three years. But had she won fairly? She was afraid he was going to take Timmy, but did she have a right to put him in jail for trying? "I'll think about it," she said.

"You have two years," the sheriff informed her.

Kari knew she had less time than that. She had until David Weeks showed up at her door, and she was sure he would. Her only hope was Gail would show up first.

* * *

The telephone rang at 2:00 p.m. Timmy was taking a nap. The events of the night before and a morning of playing outside had exhausted the boy, and Kari had insisted he "take a rest." Five minutes after she put him down, he was sound asleep.

She grabbed the phone on the first ring, afraid the sound would wake Timmy. "Kari?" Gail asked over the line.

Kari sighed in relief. "Gail. Where are you?"

"Paris." She sounded surprised by the question. "The hotel manager said you'd been calling."

"Paris?" Kari repeated, sinking into the nearest chair. All strength had left her legs, acid pouring into her stomach. "I was hoping you were on your way back. You've got to come home. David wants his son. He's going to take Timmy."

"Didn't you call the police last night?"

"Yes. I had him arrested. But this morning the sheriff's deputy said they'd let him go. He said David's not wanted for any crime, that he was cleared of those embezzlement charges and may have a right to take Timmy."

Gail swore. "Wouldn't you know it. Just when things are going great for me, too."

"You've got to come back, get a lawyer. The sheriff said, since you weren't supposed to take Timmy out of California, you might be accused of kidnapping."

"Kari, he's my own kid."

"But you weren't supposed to take him out of California."

"California . . . Michigan. He's still my kid."

"And David's," Kari reminded her.

"David gave me custody."

"Willingly?"

There was a long pause, and Kari began to wonder if they'd been disconnected. "Are you still there?"

"Yeah."

"You are coming back, aren't you?"

Again there was a pause, but she could hear Gail sigh. Holding her breath, Kari waited. She couldn't imagine Gail doing anything but coming back. They were talking about her son, her only child. Her baby.

"I can't," Gail finally said. "I can't leave now. Vernon and I, well we—I just can't leave right now."

"Vernon?" Kari couldn't believe what she was hearing.

"If I leave, I might as well forget my chances with him."

"You're willing to give up your son so you can stay with this guy?"

"It's more than that," Gail argued. "If I leave, I would also lose my job."

"There are other jobs."

"Right. At minimum wages. None would have the advantages of this one."

Kari was beginning to understand the advantages and why Gail was never in her room. "I'm sure if you explained things to Vernon, he would understand. If you talked to David face-to-face, I'm sure he would understand, too."

"And I'm sure you can convince David not to take Timmy."

"How, by telling him his ex-wife is having an affair with her boss, and that's why she can't take the time to come home for her son?"

"That was a low blow."

"Well, it's the truth, isn't it?"

"You don't understand."

"No, I don't." Kari rubbed her head, a pressure building in her temples. "Gail, Timmy needs you. I need you."

"How many times have I heard that?" she asked. "Gail, I need you to talk to my father. Gail, I need you to help me. Well, Kari, this time I need you."

Kari flinched under the reminder. "He wants his son."

"And you've got to keep him from taking him. Do whatever you have to do. If the sheriff's not going to help, call a lawyer, not that I can afford the expense."

Kari had a feeling she knew who would be absorbing the expense. Not that it mattered. Calling a lawyer was a good idea. Perhaps there was a way to legally stop David.

"And I'll talk to Vernon," Gail offered. "See if he'll let me come back in a week or two."

"Promise?"

Gail promised, and as soon as she hung up, Kari called a lawyer. Actually, she called two lawyers, first one in Bear Lake then one in Traverse City. Both stated that Gail needed to get back as soon as possible and David couldn't simply "take" Timmy. That was reassuring until the Traverse City lawyer warned her to be careful, that it wasn't uncommon for the father to kidnap the child in cases like this.

That wasn't what Kari wanted to hear. She tried calling Ralph for advice, but he was out, probably working on a client's computer, and a call to her mother brought no answer either.

Kari knew she didn't have a long time to come up with a plan. David would be coming. It was merely a question of when.

To leave Bear Lake seemed the best alternative. Leave until Gail returned. If David couldn't find Timmy, he couldn't take him. Kari called a friend from college. Marie Kraus lived in Chicago, had been a fine arts major, and now worked for an advertising firm. Marie was always inviting her to come to the city. It was time to take her up on her invitation.

As soon as the arrangements were made, Kari packed a suitcase. She grabbed the essentials in clothing and her art supplies and drawings. Two weeks away from her work would not help her meet her deadline, and Marie would understand.

Kari woke Timmy when she began stuffing his clothes and toys into a box. Sleepy-eyed, he sat on her daybed watching her as she grabbed everything Gail had brought over and explained that they were going on a little trip. It wasn't until she mentioned that Marie lived in a big city that had a museum with dinosaurs and that his mother would be back in a couple of weeks that Timmy scrambled off the bed and began helping.

All the while she packed, Kari kept listening for the sound of a car.

Her house and Maude Greene's house next door were set back from the main road, a gravel drive leading down to the parking area in front. Though the houses were old, Kari had bought hers because she liked the privacy the location afforded and the peace and quiet. Every summer tourists from downstate came up to Bear Lake to enjoy the clean air, the area's natural beauty and the lake's great fishing. The locals called them "Fudgies" because they bought the fudge that was so well-known to the area. They invaded the territory, cars jamming the main roads. The town of Bear Lake swelled in population, people all around until the cold weather descended, when the "Fudgies" would disappear like the noisy geese, heading south for milder winters. Only after the first snow did another crop of tourists return, these more interested in snowmobiling and skiing.

Maude was actually a "Fudgie," even though she'd been coming to Bear Lake for more than twenty years now. Every year she showed up on Memorial Day weekend and every year she packed her bags and said her goodbyes over Labor Day weekend. This year had been no exception. If a car came down that drive today, Kari knew the driver was either lost or coming to see her.

Today it would be David.

She had her minivan packed and had just pulled her front door shut when she saw the cream-colored car pull off the main road. Timmy was halfway between her house and her van, carrying his purple dinosaur. He stopped and watched the cream car park behind the van.

David Weeks stepped out, and acid poured into Kari's stomach, the air leaving her lungs. He looked different from the day before. The stubble of beard was gone, his hair was neatly combed and his pin-striped shirt, gray slacks and wing-tipped shoes looked new. Polished and sophisticated were words that would describe him.

Along with sexy.

She knew firsthand the sinewy strength of the corded muscles of his arms, and she'd felt the lean, hard lines of his body. Even with twenty or more feet separating them, she couldn't stop herself from responding to his innate virility. Simply looking at him caused a tightening of the muscles between her legs and an ache in her breasts. She should be afraid; what she felt was attraction.

And frustration.

She'd been so close to making her escape. Now he was blocking it.

With innocent curiosity, Timmy watched his father. It wasn't until David started toward him that Timmy turned and ran back to her, scooting behind her legs for protection.

David stopped beside her van. "Going somewhere?"

"I'm visiting a friend," Kari said, hating the quaver in her voice. How she wished she could bluff her way out, brave her way through a lie. But lying seemed foolish when he could see her suitcase and Timmy's box of clothes and toys in the back of the van.

"We're going to go see dinosaurs," Timmy added from behind her legs.

David's look was assessing, traveling from her hair, pulled back at her neck with a bright red silk scarf, down over her scoop-necked, ribbed red T-shirt, over her black jeans to her black leather shoes, then back to the black purse in her hands. "You're all ready to go?"

Again, she didn't lie. "Yes."

"You were going to leave without telling me?" He took another step toward her, and she reached down and touched the top of Timmy's head, his hair soft and warm beneath her fingertips.

"We were just going for a short visit."

Again, David glanced into her van. "Looks like you're packed for a month."

She forced a smile. "You know how it is when you travel with a child. You have to pack everything."

"No, I don't know," he said bitterly. "It's been three years since I've traveled with a child. He's my son, Kari."

"I know." She swallowed hard and watched him take another step toward them. "I can't let you take him."

"I have more right to him than you do."

"Perhaps you do, but you can't just take him. I checked with two lawyers. Each said you'll need a court order."

"And what if I have a court order?"

She hadn't banked on that. "Then…" Desperately, she searched for a reason to stop him. "David, you can't just take him. He doesn't know you. You're a stranger to him."

Which galled David. They were talking about his own son. "He'll get to know me. Timmy, come here."

He watched his son shrink farther behind Kari, fear in the boy's eyes. This wasn't the way he wanted it, his son afraid of him.

"You're scaring him," she said, taking Timmy's hand in hers. "You scared him last night."

David took another step toward the two of them, closing the gap. "I wouldn't have scared him if you hadn't made such a fuss."

"What did you expect me to do? I thought you'd escaped from prison."

"So you called in the police?" It had brought back all the nightmares, all the memories of those years of denigration.

"I did what I thought I had to do."

He believed her. He could see the fear in her eyes now. She was tense and ready for flight. If he hadn't driven up when he had, she would be gone already. "Have you talked to Gail?"

"Yes," she said warily, watching him closely. "She called this morning."

"And what did she say?"

"That she's coming back."

"Good. When?"

"My mommy's coming home in two weeks," Timmy answered boldly from behind Kari's legs.

"Two weeks, huh?"

"She can't get away until then," Kari quickly added.

He would never understand Gail, he decided. Had he been in her place, he would have been on the first plane back. She was about to lose her son, and she didn't give a damn. He looked back down at Timmy. "Your grandma and grandpa miss you."

"Grandma went to heaven," Timmy answered.

"No, your other grandma and grandpa. They live in California, where you used to live. Do you remember California?"

"California is where Billy lives."

David looked at Kari.

"I guess, from what Gail told me, Billy was Timmy's best friend," she explained.

David stooped down in front of Timmy so he was at the boy's level. "Maybe we can go see Billy again. Would you like that?"

From behind Kari's legs, Timmy nodded.

"I've missed you," David said. "Do you remember me? Do you remember your daddy?"

"No, I don't remember you. My daddy's in heaven," Timmy said firmly, hiding his face behind Kari's jeans.

"That's not true. I'm alive and I'm here and I'm going to take you back to California, where you belong. Take you back so your grandma and grandpa can see you. They've missed you."

"I don't have a daddy. I don't have a grandpa and grandma," Timmy cried, each word more agitated. "I want to go now," he insisted, pulling on Kari's hand. "I want to go see the dinosaurs."

David stood and stepped toward Timmy. Immediately Timmy began screaming, and Kari picked him up. Cuddling the child close and shielding him, she glared at David. "Is this what you want? To scare him? Terrify him?"

"I only want what's rightfully mine," David insisted.

"He's not a possession. He's a child, a little boy. He doesn't understand what's happened. He thought you were dead. He doesn't know you from the man in the moon, and now you want to take him away."

"He didn't know you, either, and Gail left him with you."

"He did know me. I'd been around Timmy for six months and he'd been over here dozens and dozens of times before Gail left him here. I made a promise to take care of him while Gail's gone. Can't you wait two weeks to do this, just until she gets back? Two weeks would give him a chance to get to know you."

"And how's he supposed to get to know me if you take him away and keep him in hiding?"

She didn't answer right away, simply stroked Timmy's head, and David knew she didn't have an answer. He wondered what lies she would come up with.

"What if I don't take him away?" she finally asked.

"And what if I don't believe you?"

She looked surprised. "You have to."

"Why?"

"Because... because we have to trust each other. You have to trust me not to take him away, and I have to be able to trust you not to take him, at least not until Gail is back."

"Which will be in two weeks?"

She hesitated slightly, then nodded. "That's what she said. You could come over here during the day and visit with Timmy, play with him. He'd learn to see you're not a threat and would get over his fear."

David shook his head.

"Why not?"

"Oh, it sounds good. Sounds perfect. Maybe too perfect."

"Meaning?"

"I've been a sucker too many times. It cost me two and a half years of my life, my reputation and my son. I'm not buying this time."

"But I'm telling you, I won't leave," she insisted. "I don't lie."

"Right." Everyone, he'd learned, lied.

"How can I convince you that I'm telling the truth?"

He had one idea. "You let me move in with you. Wherever you go, I go."

He could see her reaction to that idea in her face. Her eyes widened, growing darker until they were a cocoa brown in color, and her mouth opened in surprise. A shake of her head preceded her answer. "I won't be your prisoner. Besides, I don't have enough room."

He glanced at the house. "Looks big enough to me. What is it, three bedrooms?"

"One of which I've converted into a studio," she answered. "And believe me, there's no room in there for a person to turn around, much less sleep."

"And the other two?"

"I'm in one and Timmy's in the other. Timmy sleeps in a daybed." She grinned triumphantly. "And sometimes wets the bed."

Although David didn't think anything could be worse than a prison cell, he might make exception to that. "Which leaves sleeping with you or on your couch."

"Well, you're not sleeping with me," she said right away, but he noticed a blush of color rose to her cheeks. He also noticed she sounded a little breathless when she added, "And I don't think you'd be very comfortable on my couch . . . not for two weeks."

"All right then, any other ideas?"

For a second, she glanced at the house next door, then she looked back at him. "Perhaps one."

Chapter Four

"What's that?" David asked.

"You could stay at my neighbor's." It wasn't a perfect solution, but Kari knew it would beat having him in her house. The man exuded too much sex appeal. "Maude is gone for the winter, and she's rented her place out before. I'm sure she would rent it to you if I asked."

David looked at the two-story older home on the adjacent parcel of land. "What's to stop you from setting me up there, then taking off during the night?"

He clearly didn't trust her, not that she blamed him. He knew she'd been about to escape. Another try would seem logical. Setting Timmy down, his weight numbing her arms, she opened her front door. "So what do I have to do, give you my car keys?"

Kari held out the keys, but it was Timmy who grabbed them. With a giggle, he dashed into the house. "Timmy!" she yelled after him.

"So much for that idea," David said, a half smile

touching his lips. "Of course, I'm sure you had a spare set of keys somewhere else."

"Look, I'm not going anywhere." Not unless he forced her to flee. "Besides, if you could find Gail, I'm sure you could find me."

"Perhaps, but I don't want to spend another three months searching for my son, not when I've finally got him."

"Meaning the court order?" She didn't know what else to say or do. "May I see it?"

David wished he could show her a court order, but getting Timmy wasn't going to be as easy as he'd hoped. "I don't have it, not yet, but I've started the proceedings."

He heard Kari's sigh of relief and disliked her smile of triumph. Once again she was winning, and it galled him. "It won't take long." At least he hoped it wouldn't. "You see, I also talked to a lawyer today. She said I had a solid case, especially if I've accurately remembered the wording in the custody settlement. She's checking with my lawyer in California. I should have that court order in no time."

Kari's smile disappeared, and David noticed Timmy had come back to the doorway. "You accuse me of not thinking of my son, but you're wrong. I could have had Timmy taken from you today. The lawyer suggested having him put him in a foster home until this is settled in court."

"No," Kari gasped and looked down at Timmy. "You can't do that. Here is familiar territory for him. To take him from me and put him in a foster home..." She shook her head. "You just can't."

David admired her belief that she was doing what was best for Timmy. She was like a mother hen protecting her chick. A very lovely mother hen, he noted, the afternoon sun bringing out the tan of her cheeks and the freckles scattered across her nose.

And he couldn't really argue with her logic. To put Timmy in a foster home would be the wrong move. "As I said, she suggested I put him in one. I didn't agree. Not that I think his being with you is the way it should be. By all rights, right now Timmy and I should be on our way back to California."

"No!" Timmy yelled, and backing into the house, he slammed the door shut.

Kari turned and found herself facing solid wood, and before she could reach for the doorknob, she heard the clunk of the lock. Stunned, she tried it, then looked at David. "He's locked us out."

"Timmy, let us in," David ordered, coming up beside her.

"No. Go away!" Timmy yelled through the door. "Go away, both of you. I want my mommy."

"Your mommy isn't here," David said. His arm brushed against Kari's, and she looked up at him. For a moment she saw a flicker of awareness in his blue gaze, then Timmy yelled again, and David looked away.

"You're not my daddy," Timmy shouted through the door.

The boy was getting hysterical, and she knew she needed to say something...do something. "Yes, he is your daddy," she called back. "I can show you some pictures of when you were a baby and he was holding you."

"Really?" David mouthed, and she nodded.

It was Timmy who didn't believe her. "Mommy said my daddy went to heaven."

"Well, I've come back." David shook his head. "He's a stubborn kid, isn't he?"

"Like his father," Kari answered.

She was delighted by David's grin. It played across his face, relaxing his features and bringing a sparkle to his eyes. "Any good ideas?" he asked.

She nodded and backed away from the door. "You keep him talking."

"What should I say?"

"I don't care, just keep him talking."

David dug back into his memory. "I remember the day you were born," he said to the door. "The doctor let me be right there. He didn't have to spank you. No, sirree, you came out hollering."

"I don't believe you," Timmy said, but the edge was gone from his voice.

David went on as though nothing had been said. "You were a good baby. Didn't cry a lot. For a while there I thought you were just going to sleep and eat and wet your diapers. Your mommy used to sing to you. I loved listening to her sing. Does she still sing to you?"

"Sometimes," Timmy said solemnly. "Mommy says I cry too much now."

"Why do you cry?" David asked. Anything he could use against Gail would help him in his fight for Timmy.

"'Cause...I can hold my breath under water. Can you?"

"Only for a little while. Why do you cry, Timmy?"

"'Cause I miss Billy. 'Cause I want you to go away. I want everyone to go away. I want—"

David knew something had cut Timmy off, but it wasn't until Kari opened the door, a wiggling four-year-old in her arms, that he understood. "How'd you get inside?"

"Back door. I never lock my doors." She grunted when Timmy hit at her. "Okay, that is enough." Setting him on his feet, she pointed toward the back of her house. "I know this is hard for you, but we don't hit. Now, go to your room. When you calm down, you may come out."

Timmy stomped through her living room, into her kitchen and then turned to his right. David flinched when the bedroom door slammed. Kari sighed. "I can't let you take him."

"Give me one reason why not?"

"Gail." She managed a smile. "I promised her I'd keep Timmy with me until she got back. Like you, I believe in that 'for better or worse' clause."

"Your loyalty is commendable." He stepped closer. "You could tell her I overpowered you and took him from you."

The thought of him putting his arms around her again, holding her close, sent a quivery sensation flowing through her. Her breath locked in her chest, and Kari could only shake her head.

"Then it looks like I stay."

She saw his gaze move to the couch behind her, then to the open door to her bedroom. "No," she managed, disturbed by how faint her voice sounded.

His smile was too suggestive, the glint in his eyes teasing. "All right, then," he said, "give your neighbor a call."

It took a while for Kari to explain to Maude everything that had happened, but by the time she hung up, Maude had agreed to lease her house to David for as long as he needed it. Kari hoped she hadn't made the biggest mistake of her life.

"Now you two can come with me while I check out of my motel," David said.

Kari faced him. "That was not part of our deal."

"It's part of my deal."

"Then the deal's off. Either you trust me or we forget this."

"And when I get back...?"

"We'll be here. You have my word, remember?"

"The question is, how good is your word?"

"Here's your chance to find out."

He stared at her, and she knew he was trying to decide if he could trust her. She knew she didn't trust him. He wanted his son, and she had a feeling he'd go to any lengths to get him. Finally, he shook his head and started for her front door. "I think I'm making a mistake."

She knew she was.

Kari waited until David had driven off before she knocked on Timmy's door. "He's gone," she said and peeked into the room. "You all right?"

Timmy sat on his bed cross-legged, his purple dinosaur cuddled under his chin, his big blue eyes filled with tears. "He's not my daddy."

She chose not to argue. "I'm going to unload the van. Do you want to help?"

"I wanna go see the dinosaurs."

"So do I," she admitted and sat beside Timmy. She wanted to be anywhere but around David. He made her feel guilty.

He made her feel quivery.

"So can we go?" Timmy climbed down from the daybed and looked back at her.

"No." She'd made a promise. She'd made too many promises. "We can't go." Standing, she started for the door. "We have to stay here until your mother gets back and works this out with your father."

"Then I'm not going to help you." He pouted and climbed back onto the bed, and she wondered if she would ever regain his trust.

Leaving Timmy in his room, she went outside. The bright sunlight of earlier that day was rapidly giving way to dark storm clouds that echoed her dismal mood. Below the clouds a gaggle of geese flew in a V formation, calling to one another. To take flight sounded so good. To leave Bear Lake and all her problems. To head south. Head anywhere.

"Take me with you," she called to the geese.

The geese flew on, and she sighed. "Maybe I'll write a book about a little girl faced with lots of problems who flies away."

She might as well get something out of this ordeal.

David watched from behind the massive trunk of the maple tree growing at the top of her drive. He'd expected to see her come out of her house with Timmy. He was sure she was going to take off. It was what he would do.

He hadn't expected her to talk to geese. The lady was certifiable...and absolutely adorable. He remembered how she'd felt in his arms, so small and vibrant. He hadn't meant to scare her last night, but she was a fighter. His son was facing a losing battle if he thought he was going to get the best of Kari Carmichael.

David had a feeling *he* was facing a losing battle.

He watched her wheel her suitcase back to her house, the sun catching the reddish highlights of her hair. He could almost smell the flowery scent of her shampoo, feel the silky texture of each strand. Her ponytail bounced and wiggled, and his gaze drifted down to her jeans. The age-softened denim hugged the curve of her bottom, teasing him.

A tightening in his loins told him it was a good thing he wouldn't be staying at her house. If simply looking at her was arousing feelings he shouldn't be having, what would sleeping near her arouse? He might be here for his son, but he wasn't immune to a pretty woman.

When she carried Timmy's box back into the house, David decided she wasn't leaving. Making sure he wasn't seen, he worked his way back to his car. She'd said he could trust her.

For the moment, it seemed he could.

Kari was standing by her van when David returned. She'd been waiting for him. At the sound of gravel crunching under his tires, she pulled her portfolio out and slid the door closed, hoping he would think the timing was accidental. She waited until he was out of his car, then called to him. "Can I talk to you for a minute?"

"Sure." He closed his door and walked over. A breeze caught several strands of hair on his forehead, pulling them up like golden threads. She was growing more accustomed to seeing him, of thinking of him as alive. What she was finding difficult was thinking of him as Gail's husband.

Ex-husband, she told herself, yet knew it shouldn't matter. If he'd married Gail, he wouldn't be interested in her. Gail and she were as different as night and day, as dark and light. She was the shy one, the quiet one. Gail had always been the shining star. It was blond, green-eyed models with long legs, buxom chests and beautiful faces who attracted men like David Weeks. Short, plain, brown-eyed brunettes attracted the Ralph Schneiders of the world.

Kari started haltingly. "I know you see me as the enemy."

He merely smiled, but it sent ripples of excitement through her and made it more difficult for her to think straight. "And I don't know what happened between you and Gail."

"My loving wife deserted me," he said simply. "When I needed her, she wasn't there."

"I'm sorry about that. And I'm sorry about what happened last night. If I'd known—"

David frowned. "Do you have any idea how humiliating it is to be handcuffed and carted off like an animal?"

"I didn't know what else to do. I was scared you were going to take Timmy. I'm still scared you're going to take him."

"He was taken from me." David couldn't stop himself from reaching out and touching her arm. Her skin was as velvety soft and warm as he remembered.

Immediately she tensed.

It wasn't the reaction he wanted. "Don't be afraid of me, Kari. I'm not going to hurt you."

Looking into his eyes, Kari knew that wasn't true. He could hurt her. He could make her care what happened to him, make her want what she couldn't have. His only interest was his son. She had to remember that.

She moved her arm, breaking contact. "I want to talk to you about Timmy," Kari said, getting her mind back on track. "I know you're upset because he keeps denying you're his father, but you have to realize, it's going to take time. Don't push him. Let him come to you."

"How much time?"

"I don't know," she said honestly. "He's been with me for a week. He was really upset when Gail first left, but he's been getting much better."

"Until I showed up?"

"Yes." She looked toward her house. "What I'd like to suggest is you have dinner with us tonight. As long as I have to cook for two, I might as well cook for three. When you see him, don't say anything about taking him away. If anything, ignore him." She laughed. "He hates that. He's like Gail in that way, always has to be center stage."

"So what time is dinner?"

Kari gave David a quick tour of Maude's house, left him with the key, then returned to her house and started dinner. It wasn't much: frozen steaks broiled in the oven, mashed potatoes and peas. David came over at six o'clock. To her surprise, he was carrying a brass lamp. "To replace the one I broke last night," he said.

"You didn't have to." She took it from him, certain he'd paid far more for this one than she had for the one he'd broken. "It was my fault more than yours. You wouldn't have broken it if I hadn't tried to hit you with it."

"Either way." He stepped past her into her living room. Stopping near the couch, he looked around.

She wondered if he was remembering the events of the night before or if it was the house itself he was noticing for the first time. Four years ago, Gail had sent her a long letter describing the house David had bought for her. It had sounded like a mansion. Kari knew, by comparison, her place must look like a dump. Her parents certainly didn't think much of it. The house was old, and most of her furnishings were from the Goodwill store, the only discernible decor being no decor.

"It's not much, but it's home," she said, taking the lamp over to the table the other lamp had been on.

"I like it. It feels homey," he said, watching her.

"Someday, when I either write or illustrate that bestseller and am raking in the millions, I'll be able to fix it up with furniture that matches." She laughed. "But that might be a while."

He shook his head. "As I said, looks fine to me."

She wasn't sure why his approval should please her so, but it did. Feeling ready to take on the world—and Timmy—she headed for the kitchen.

Timmy stayed as far away from David as he could and made a fuss when it came time to sit down for dinner. Kari insisted he join them at the table, but allowed him to move his chair to the opposite end.

As they ate, she and David talked about the weather in northern Michigan, about the town of Bear Lake and about the lake itself. Not once did David say anything to Timmy. He rarely even looked at his son, and she had to suppress a grin when Timmy began trying to get David's attention.

Finally David gave a sign of recognition, and Timmy launched into a dissertation on the history of dinosaurs, from a four-year-old's point of view. Kari was actually ready to hang out her shingle in child psychology. Everything seemed perfect. Son was getting to know father, and father was getting to know son.

And then Timmy started playing with his mashed potatoes, and David told him to stop.

"You can't tell me what to do," Timmy said, glaring at David. "You know what you are? You're a . . ."

Timmy let loose with a string of swear words that amazed Kari, with toilet functions seemingly his preferred venue. David pushed back his chair, and Kari was afraid of what he might do. Quickly she said, "Timothy Patrick Weeks, I do not allow that kind of talk in my house. If you are finished eating, you will leave this table and go wash your hands."

"Better wash your mouth while you're at it," David added.

Still glaring at him, Timmy pushed his fork into his mashed potatoes, and Kari was sure he was going to fling the pile at David. "Don't you dare," she warned.

He looked at her, his glare daring her to do anything.

"Didn't I tell you to go wash your hands?"

"You can't make me," Timmy said defiantly. "You're not my mommy."

"Oh, yes I can." If it was going to be a battle of wills, she was determined not to lose. "Your mommy left you under my care, and in my house, if you play with your food, you're finished eating. Now, go wash your hands."

Timmy dropped the fork back on the plate with a clank. "I want a cookie."

"No cookies," she said.

Once again, Timmy began swearing.

"I will not . . ." David stood, but Kari stopped him with a shake of her head.

"Go wash your hands," she repeated.

Timmy glared at the two of them, measuring David's height and her determination. Then, pouting, he got down from his chair and stomped into the bathroom, slamming the door behind him. David grimaced and sat back down, his shoulders sagging.

Timmy's behavior didn't bother her as much as David's. "Would you have hit him?"

"Timmy?" He frowned at the idea. "No, but if he hadn't gone into that bathroom on his own, he was going to get a little help. Is he always like this?"

"No." She leaned back in her chair, the tension leaving her body. She didn't like confrontations of any kind, not even with a four-year-old. "There are times when he's an absolute delight. So imaginative and playful. And he can really be loving." She smiled, remembering the night before David had shown up, when Timmy had given her a big hug. "He's going to be a real heartbreaker when he grows up."

A lot like you, she thought, looking at David. "He already knows his numbers, so maybe he'll also be an accountant."

She didn't get the smile from David that she'd expected. Instead, he shook his head. "I hope he's a smarter accountant than his father."

She was pretty sure he was thinking of the embezzlement charges and the time he'd spent in prison. "Was being in jail rough?"

He shrugged. "Not as bad as it could have been, I guess. It was a white-collar crime. Minimum security. It was the lack of freedom that got to me. Being taken away from my family. Not being able to see my own son. He's changed so much, grown so much."

"He's grown in the six months I've known him," Kari said. "I have some pictures I took when he first got here. Oh, yes, and those of you and Timmy." She rose from her chair. "I'll get them."

She went into the living room and had started toward her bookcase when she glanced out her front window and saw Ralph Schneider's blue car coming down the drive. His timing couldn't have been worse. Glancing toward her kitchen, she decided the best thing was to head Ralph off at the pass.

Kari went outside. The sky was now completely gray and the temperature had dropped considerably. She hadn't changed from the short-sleeved top she'd had on earlier or slipped on a sweater. The moment the wind hit her, she wished she had. Waiting for Ralph, she wrapped her arms across her chest, hoping to conserve heat.

He got out of his car and waved. "Thought I'd stop by."

"Not the best of timing," she said. "Timmy's having a temper tantrum, and I'm going to have to get him ready for bed."

Her message didn't get through, and Ralph started toward her. His reddish blond hair looked long overdue for a cut, and a lock dropped down across his forehead to touch the rim of his glasses. He wasn't what she would call handsome, and he always made her feel as if she should feed him to get some weight on his bones, but he was a nice person. Steadfast and intelligent did describe him, as much as Kari hated to admit it. He was a real genius when it came to computers. She liked him; however, in the ten months she'd been dating him, she couldn't remember any time he'd ever made her feel "quivery" inside. Comfortable was a better word to describe her feelings around Ralph.

"You okay after last night?" he asked.

"Fine." She really didn't want to discuss it, not with David in the house. "I overreacted."

"From what I heard, you did the right thing. I was at the sheriff's office today, working on one of their computers. One of the deputies said you were thinking of filing assault charges against the guy."

"I didn't say that." She didn't want Ralph spreading rumors.

"Well, I think you should. My gosh, Kari, the guy attacked you. He—"

Ralph stopped, his gaze moving past her to a point beyond. She had a feeling she knew *what* he was looking at—or rather *whom*. Turning, she faced her house.

Her front door was now open, David standing on her stoop, his hands on his hips, and his expression guarded.

Ralph came up beside her. "What's he doing here?"

"Visiting his son."

She wasn't sure when David had stepped out of her house or how much of her conversation with Ralph he'd overheard. She didn't want any misunderstanding. Looking at him, she explained. "They said I could file charges against you. I'm not."

"I suppose I should thank you." He kept his gaze on Ralph.

"This is Ralph Schneider. He's a good friend, and an absolute genius when it comes to computers," she said, positioning herself between the two men. "And Ralph, this is David Weeks, Timmy's father and Gail's ex-husband." She didn't add that he was going to be her next-door neighbor for a while.

David came down her steps and shook hands with Ralph. The gesture was friendly, but Kari could feel a tension between the two men. "Planning on working on her computer tonight?" David asked, stepping back beside her.

The gesture wasn't lost on Ralph, and he kept his gaze on her when he answered. "No, I thought I'd stop by and make sure she was all right after what you did to her last night."

"And just what did she say I did to her?"

"Nothing," Kari answered, shivering in the cold. "I haven't said anything."

"Just what *did* he do to you?" Ralph demanded, glaring at David.

"Nothing," she repeated. "I told you this morning, it was all a big misunderstanding."

And she had a feeling tonight was going to turn into another big misunderstanding. She was having a hard enough time herself trying to understand what was happening. How could she hope to explain it to Ralph? And even though, in the ten months they'd been going out, Ralph had kept their relationship casual, asking for no more than a good-night kiss, she knew it was generally acknowledged around town that they were a couple. He wasn't going to like what she was doing.

Again, she shivered, and David moved even closer, slipping an arm around her shoulders. "You should have put on a sweater. You're freezing."

Another shiver traveled through her, but this time Kari knew it had nothing to do with the cold. The weight of his arm and the warmth of his body had her tingling from head to toes, and breathing was suddenly an impossibility. He was touching her . . . and she liked it.

Ralph glared at David but spoke to her. "What's going on, Kari?"

"Nothing," she argued, too confused by her feelings to move.

"Nothing," David agreed. Smiling, he looked at her. "We just finished dinner, and she was going to show me some pictures. Weren't you?"

"Dinner?" Ralph focused on her. "You invited this man over for dinner?"

Kari knew he was getting the wrong impression. Moving away from David, she tried to explain. "Gail had told Timmy his father was dead, and I'm trying to get Timmy to accept David as his father. I figured, since David had to eat—"

Ralph interrupted. "The man also has to sleep. Will you be inviting him to spend the night?"

David answered for her. "She wouldn't let me spend the night, but she did set me up next door."

Ralph switched his gaze to Maude's house. "He's living there . . . next to you?"

"So he can get to know his son. So Timmy can get to know him. It's only for two weeks. Gail's coming back then."

"Maude let an ex-con rent her house?"

She couldn't let Ralph go around town telling people David was an ex-con. "He was cleared of those charges. He was proved innocent."

"Not everyone believes that. Deputy Walker said it sounded fishy to him."

"Deputy Walker had better watch what he says," David snapped. "If he starts spreading rumors, he's going to be facing a lawsuit."

Kari knew David was also threatening Ralph with one if those rumors started, and that any accusations of guilt hurt him. She'd glimpsed his pain the night before. It was bad enough that he'd been imprisoned for almost three years for a crime he hadn't committed. He didn't need complete strangers questioning his innocence.

"He's innocent, Ralph," she repeated. "And I think you'd better come back another time. Timmy really did throw a temper tantrum, and I think he's still in the bathroom. I need to check on him and get him ready for bed. I'll give you a call tomorrow and explain everything."

"You do that," Ralph said curtly and once again glared at David.

She didn't wait for Ralph to leave or David to move. Ignoring both men, she headed for her bathroom. The moment she stepped into her house, she could hear the pump running. Before she reached the bathroom door, she saw the water running out from under the threshold.

Chapter Five

"Oh, no," Kari said with a groan.

Timmy sat on the floor beneath the bathroom sink, not a stitch of clothing on his body, water cascading down over his head and shoulders to the linoleum floor. He looked up at her through the nearly white wet hair hanging over his eyes, a wide grin covering his face. "Look, Aunt Kari. I'm taking a shower."

For a moment Kari could only stare. Never in her imagination had she thought taking care of a four-year-old would involve so much energy. Her first impulse was to yell, her second to cry, and then she began to laugh. Stepping into the room, her shoes immediately soaking up water, she turned off the faucets. "No more shower."

"What the...?" she heard from behind and half turned to look at David. He stood near the doorway, staring at the water on the floor and at his son.

"Timmy decided to take a shower."

"By running the water in the sink?"

"Never underestimate the imagination of a child." She motioned with a hand. "In the closet just to your right there are towels. Grab a bunch."

Kari helped Timmy to his feet. "You take one and dry yourself off."

"I wanna help," Timmy insisted.

"Then help," David said, tossing a towel Timmy's way. "My mother was a firm believer if you made a mess, you cleaned it up."

A good idea, Kari decided. A few more minutes of nudity wouldn't hurt Timmy. Her house wasn't that cool.

They worked as a team, Timmy and she using the towels to soak up the water, David taking them from them and squeezing out the water in the tub before handing them back. Timmy didn't seem to realize he was working within inches of his father, nor did he seem to mind when David warned him to be careful. And when they were nearly finished, Timmy squealed with glee when David snapped a towel at him.

One hour later, the bathroom was relatively dry, a space heater finishing the job; Timmy had been readied for bed and read to and a relative calm had settled over the house. Her clothes were damp from splashed and dripping water, but Kari was too tired to care. Sinking onto her living room couch, she sighed.

David stood in the middle of the room, large dampened areas covering his shirt and slacks, his sleeves rolled to his elbows, and his shoes and socks off. Without thinking, she patted the cushion beside her. "You as tired as I am?"

He chuckled as he eased himself onto the couch, keeping a respectable distance between them. "Does he always have that much energy?"

"Always."

She closed her eyes, her long lashes brushing her cheeks, and David let himself enjoy her gentle beauty. She'd amazed him earlier. Most women, he was sure, would have had a fit if they'd found that much water on their floor. Instead, Kari had laughed, and the entire cleanup had turned into a game.

She was a puzzle in herself. She certainly wasn't the shy little mouse Gail had described, though there were signs of that shyness: the downward cast of her eyes when he offered a compliment, her quiet voice and the solitude of her work. She also didn't talk a lot; periods of silence didn't seem to bother her. On the other hand, she didn't hesitate to speak up if her integrity was questioned or when she was arguing on Gail's behalf.

Two more opposite women he couldn't have imagined.

His gaze drifted down from Kari's face to her water-dampened top. No, Kari Carmichael did not have his ex-wife's measurements. Nor her height. Nor her stunning presence. Men never failed to notice Gail. He wondered how many men had overlooked Kari.

One, evidently, hadn't. "You should have mentioned that you had a boyfriend."

She opened her eyes and looked at him. "You mean Ralph?" Quickly, she glanced away. "I guess the opportunity just never came up."

"What I did out there, putting my arm around you, that was stupid." He still didn't understand what had prompted the action, other than he could tell she was cold, and somehow he'd wanted to warm her.

She said nothing, simply stared down at her carpeting.

"Have you been going out with him long?"

"Ten months."

"Then it's serious?" Why that bothered him was even more troubling.

"I don't know." She looked at him again, frowning. "He's a nice guy. Really smart when it comes to computers. And I've really enjoyed going out with him."

"But no bells, no fireworks?"

Kari grinned. "Is that how it was with you and Gail?"

"It was for me." He sighed, remembering. "I guess that song's right—'Fools Rush In.' I was a fool to believe her lies. A fool to marry her so quickly."

"Were you a fool to have Timmy?"

He shook his head. "Timmy's the one good thing that came out of that union."

"Which reminds me..." She pushed herself up from the couch. "I'll show you those pictures."

They looked at pictures of David and Timmy, David and Gail, Timmy and Gail and Timmy by himself. David's responses to the pictures of Gail were all negative, but he studied the ones of Timmy with an intensity that touched Kari. It was as if he wanted to absorb each photo, reach back in time to that point in Timmy's life. She could sense his sadness.

When David left, she carried that sadness with her to bed. Long into the night she thought of him looking at those pictures, of him snapping the towel at Timmy while they mopped up the bathroom, and of him slipping his arm around her shoulders when they were talking to Ralph.

Maybe it wasn't bells she'd heard, but he had brought the fireworks. The explosion had been in her head, or maybe her heart. No touch by Ralph had ever created such a warmth or excitement. No two days with Ralph had ever been so exciting.

That bothered her.

When Kari's phone rang the next morning, she expected it to be Ralph. Not wanting to discuss the events of the night before in front of Timmy, she answered the call in her studio. She hadn't thought it might be Gail, nor had she imagined what Gail might have to say.

"What do you mean you aren't coming back in two weeks?" Kari said, dumbfounded.

"I can't," Gail insisted. "You have to understand. I can't leave until we're finished here. Vernon is everything I've ever wanted in a man, and he thinks I'm wonderful. He's taking me to Switzerland this weekend, and he's taking about us going to the French Riviera for Thanksgiving. If I left now... Well, I just can't. Too much depends on my staying."

"What about your son?" Gail had barely even asked about Timmy.

"I'm doing this for him. This job and Vernon can guarantee us a decent future."

"You won't have a future with Timmy if David takes him."

"But you just said he couldn't do that until he gets a court order, and that he'd agreed to stick around and let Timmy get to know him."

"For two weeks. That's all he agreed to, Gail. Fourteen days. And he only agreed to that because I told him you were coming back."

"So I'll be gone a little longer than expected." She didn't sound the least bit concerned. "David's staying next door?"

"Yes. Maude said he could lease her place as long as he needed."

"There's a phone over there, isn't there? One that's working?"

"It's working." Kari remembered David mentioning that he'd gotten a call from some telemarketer only an hour after moving his things in.

"Give me the number," Gail said. "I'll call him. I was always able to talk David into anything."

She laughed, and Kari wondered exactly what Gail had talked David into. After she hung up, she wondered what Gail had talked her into. To watch Timmy was one thing. The idea of being around David for an extended period of time was another.

* * *

David slammed down the phone and swore. If Gail thought he'd bought her hard-luck story, she really took him for a fool. Her "bound by a contract to stay the full three months" was so full of holes, it was pitiful. Contracts, he knew, could be broken.

She'd certainly broken their marriage contract.

"I can hardly wait to see you again," she'd said so sweetly.

He'd see her all right. In court. And if he could legally do it, it would be in a California courtroom.

Everything would depend on what he heard from the lawyer he'd talked to yesterday. If she—

He heard a door slam and glanced out the window. He could see Timmy running from Kari's house toward the stream that cut through the two backyards. A half-dozen sleeping ducks rose to their feet, flapping their wings and quacking in alarm, but none flew away. Then he heard Kari, the sound of her voice barely reaching through the closed window. Automatically, he looked her way.

She stood by her back door, a bulky jacket and slacks covering her body and leather boots on her feet. The wind caught her hair, blowing it across her face like a wispy veil, and she brushed it back, then said something to Timmy.

He stopped a few feet from the ducks and began tossing grain from a coffee can he held. The ducks ceased their commotion and waddled closer, snatching the grain from the grass.

David smiled as he watched his son, the tension slowly easing from his shoulders and his anger tapering to reason. If Gail thought her staying away would impede his getting custody of Timmy, she was sorely mistaken. He would have preferred taking Timmy back to California with him, but if he had to stick around here for an eternity to get his son, he would. The only problem was going to be money.

Timmy ran back to where Kari stood, his red jacket open. She zipped it up, then turned back toward her house. David thought she was going inside, but instead she covered her eyes with her arm. At first concerned, he watched, then he realized what was happening.

Timmy darted off, heading for three young pine trees about four feet in height. Crouching behind one, he hid.

Hide-and-seek.

David hadn't played it for years.

Fascinated, he watched Kari slowly turn around and begin looking. Timmy's red jacket showed through the green boughs of the pines, but Kari went in the opposite direction, looking inside the small toolshed close to the edge of her house, behind the shed, up trees and under bushes. She looked everywhere but where Timmy was hiding.

He couldn't hear anything being said, but he knew she was talking, probably cajoling Timmy to show himself. David remembered the sound of her voice from the night before. Sitting next to her, looking at the pictures she had, he'd found himself enjoying the softness of her tone. He wouldn't call hers a sexy voice. Certainly not like Gail's. More...

He groped for a word and came up with "appealing." Yes, her voice was appealing. To be honest, *she* was appealing. Cute. Small. Vulnerable-looking but feisty. It was going to be difficult for him to remember, no matter what she said, it was not he or his best interest she was concerned about. She was Gail's friend. There was where her allegiance would be.

She finally "found" Timmy, her gestures ones of surprise. All women, David decided, were consummate liars. Timmy laughed, his entire body expressing his delight, and Kari crouched in front of him and gave him a hug. It was all very touching, but David wondered if she was aware that he was watching. Was she simply putting on a show? After talking to Gail, he was suspicious.

He grabbed his own jacket, the lightweight nylon inadequate for the drop in temperature from the day before but his only choice. Zipping it up, he headed outside. Timmy saw him first. His smile was tentative but there, and David knew they'd made some progress the night before.

Kari also smiled when she stood and faced him, yet he saw a tension in her. He knew why. She was in on Gail's little game.

He forced himself to pretend all was fine. "Whatcha playing?" he asked Timmy.

The boy stayed close to Kari. "Hide-and-seek," he said, looking up at her for reassurance.

"And he's very good at it," Kari said, ruffling the boy's hair. She glanced at David's jacket. "You're going to need something warmer than that today."

"It will do." He didn't plan on staying out long. "I just got off the phone. I'm sure you can't imagine who I was talking to."

He knew from her expression of guilt that she did, and she quickly glanced down at Timmy. "Think you can pull out those dead flowers by my back door? I'll pay you a dime."

Timmy looked at her flower bed, then up at her. "I wanna nickel. Nickels are bigger."

"Ooh, you drive a hard bargain." She smiled and nodded. "A nickel it is."

She waited until Timmy had run to the flower bed, then turned back to David. "We've been playing banker. He's having a little trouble learning the value of money."

"And I'm having a little trouble figuring out what your game is."

"Game?" Her expression became guarded. "I don't understand?"

"Gail said you've been lying to me."

"She said *I've* been lying to you?" Kari's eyes flashed her surprise.

"I don't know what else you would call your telling me that she'd be back in two weeks. She said she never said any such thing, that she can't because of that penalty clause in her contract."

"What penalty clause in her contract?" Kari asked, then corrected herself. "I mean, I guess I wasn't aware of one."

She looked down, avoiding eye contact. He cradled her chin in one hand, lifting her face so she had to look at him. "You don't lie as well as Gail does."

"May be because I don't lie." She glared at him. "If Gail told me about a penalty clause, I don't remember."

"Why didn't you take off yesterday when I went to get my things? Did you suspect I was watching?"

"No, I did not suspect you were watching." She pushed his hand away, the look in her brown eyes icy. "I didn't think you'd stoop that low."

"And how low will you stoop, Kari Carmichael? When will you disappear with my son?"

"Any minute," she said frigidly, "if you keep this up."

He stared at her, not so sure she wouldn't. Her chin high and her spine rigid, she reminded him of his mother when he'd pushed her too far. He released his frustration with a chuckle. "You are not the Miss Milquetoast Gail described."

"And you are not the sweet, loving husband she described to me."

"A transformation of character that I owe entirely to my loving wife's lack of fidelity and my best friend's lack of honesty."

"So now, because of what you've been through and the injustice you've suffered, it's okay to bully your way through life, take what isn't yours, is that it?"

"Timmy is mine."

"He is not a possession, he's a child," she reminded him.

"My child."

"And Gail's."

He looked over to where Timmy was pulling up Kari's dead marigolds. "Have you told him she's not coming back in two weeks?"

"No." David heard her sigh. "He wouldn't understand. At his age, time—like money—has no meaning. Two weeks can seem as long as two and a half months."

She looked back at him. "For an adult, two and a half months can be a short time."

"If an adult has unlimited funds." Which he didn't, not if he was going to be paying more lawyer and court fees.

"Do you have a job waiting back in California?" she asked.

He laughed at the idea. "Who's had time to look for a job? I've spent all of my time, and a good percentage of the money I had left, trying to track down my son."

"Is there any reason why you absolutely have to be back in California right away?"

He thought of his parents. "My folks would like to see their grandson."

"I'm sure they will, soon." She touched the sleeve of his jacket. "All we're asking for is a little time. Time for Timmy to get to know you. Time for Gail to get back. I think I know where you could find a job."

"Where?" he asked, certain she had a trick up her sleeve.

"At the Bear Lake Resort. It's just outside of town, at the base of Bear Mountain. People stay there to golf or cross-country ski or just to enjoy the countryside. Ralph was there last week, working on their computers, and he said they've lost a lot of employees, including an accountant. You're still an accountant, aren't you?"

"Yes." But that didn't mean someone would hire him. And he wasn't sure getting a job would be a good idea. "While I'm off working, where will you be? Timbuktu?"

"Right here. I have illustrations to finish, a newsletter to get out for one of the local merchants, and my publisher has been bugging me to come up with an idea for a book. I can't be running around the countryside, hiding from you."

"You were about to yesterday," he reminded her.

"That was when I thought Gail would be back in two weeks."

He was beginning to believe her, which bothered him. Either he'd been wrong and she was a consummate liar, or he wasn't the only one Gail was jerking around. "Okay, let's say I go and I get this job at the resort. What then?"

"You work during the day, get to know Timmy evenings and weekends, and when Gail gets back, the two of you can work this out together."

"There's nothing to work out. She broke the custody agreement, took him out of the state without permission and left him with a stranger while she ran off to Paris with some guy."

"She did not run off with some guy. She's in Paris with her boss. She's there on business," Kari insisted, though she knew business was only half the reason Gail was there.

"If you believe that, you are very naive."

She glared at him, her eyes narrowing. "Are you going to do it or not?"

He hesitated, looking over at Timmy. The boy certainly wasn't going to go with him willingly, not at this point. And to take him might jeopardize his legal position.

"If I get the job," he said finally, "I'll stick around until Gail returns."

* * *

Three days later, Kari nervously glanced at the clock in her kitchen. It was almost two. David's interview had been scheduled for one o'clock. He should be through.

"Can I have another cookie, Aunt Kari?" Timmy asked, a ring of white milk around his mouth.

"Sure. Then it's time for a rest." She'd found it better to call it a rest than a nap.

"I'm not tired," he argued.

"But you still need to rest." And she needed time to work on her paintings...if she could work. She'd been tense all day, her mind always wandering back to David and this job. He had to get it. If he didn't, she wasn't sure what he might do.

She heard a car and immediately went into her living room. Through the window she saw David's car, and something inside of her stomach twisted. He parked in front of Maude's and got out, straightening the jacket of his suit before closing the door to his car.

She watched him walk toward her place, his stride slow and his head down. He didn't look like a man who'd just gotten a job. He also didn't look like the man who'd barged into her house less than a week ago. He was now clean-shaven, his blond hair had been neatly trimmed, and his navy pin-striped suit looked fresh and new.

Which it was, since he'd bought it only the day before.

She checked her own hair, running her fingers through it to pull out any tangles, and glanced down at her sweats. She should have changed, she told herself, should have put on something less grungy. But then she chastised herself for the thought. She wasn't trying to impress him. He was Gail's ex-husband and Timmy's father. He wasn't coming over to see her, at least not in a romantic way. He came over only because she had Timmy.

Kari opened her front door before he'd made it up her concrete steps. Fingers crossed behind her back, she asked, "How'd it go?"

He shrugged dejectedly, each step slowly bringing him closer, but she thought she saw a glint of amusement in the blue of his eyes and just the hint of a smile. And then he stopped in front of her, his head came up, and his mouth captured a full-fledged smile. "I got it."

Relief swept over Kari, the weight on her shoulders suddenly gone. Grinning, she motioned for him to come in. "That's great. What did you say? What did they say? Tell me everything."

He surprised her by laughing, the sound rumbling from deep down in his chest. "Well," he began. "Don Wilkerson, the resort's owner, was there. I guess he's normally not around but he'd flown up to look over the place. I really didn't think I was going to get the job. Wilkerson kept asking me questions about the embezzlement charges and my acquittal. And then Peterson—Wayne Peterson, he's the resort's manager—wanted to know how much I knew about computers, and I had to admit I could run most spreadsheets, but I didn't know all that much about the computer itself. I figured he was looking for someone who did know computers inside and out, so when they asked me to step outside and wait, I was sure I could kiss the job goodbye. You can imagine my surprise when they called me back in and Wilkerson said I had the job if I wanted it."

"And, of course, you told them you'd think about it."

"I start Monday. Where's Timmy?"

"In the kitchen. We were having cookies and milk." She grinned. "Would you like to join us?"

"Sounds delightful."

"Cookies any good?" he asked Timmy as he went to the cookie jar and pulled out one for himself.

Timmy said nothing, simply looked at him.

"Guess what, son? I got a job today."

Kari stayed back by the doorway, wanting Timmy to relate with his father. David didn't crowd the boy. He stayed on the opposite side of the counter and didn't make any gestures toward Timmy. Nevertheless, Timmy scooted off his stool, cookie in hand, and ran to his bedroom. David grimaced the same time she did when Timmy's door slammed. Then he looked her way and smiled wanly. "I guess he wasn't impressed."

She knew what the problem was. Five minutes of talking to his mother had made Timmy moody again. "Give him time," she said. She walked over to the sink and grabbed a rag to wipe up the crumbs Timmy had left on the counter.

David watched her. "I saw your boyfriend today."

She looked up. "Ralph?"

"How many boyfriends do you have?"

"Just Ralph." She wasn't even sure he was a boyfriend. The two times they'd talked since he'd stopped by, Ralph had been cool and distant... almost irritable.

"He made it clear he wasn't pleased I'm living next door to you."

"What did he say?" She certainly hadn't expected Ralph to harass David.

"Just that he's not pleased that I'm living next door to you."

The smile that quirked David's mouth said Ralph had said more or at least that Ralph hadn't worded it quite as politely. She wasn't sure if she should be pleased or irritated. "We've never made any commitment to each other. He has no right to bother you."

"I think he'd like a right, and I don't think he's going to like me spending time over here. Or do you plan on letting me keep Timmy next door with me after I get home from work?"

She really hadn't thought about how they would work that part out. "I don't think Timmy would stay with you right now. Gail talked to him today."

David frowned and looked at the closed bedroom door. "Well, that at least explains his behavior. What did she tell him, that I eat little boys?"

"I don't know what she said." Timmy wouldn't tell Kari. "David, I don't like what she's doing. It's just that—"

"What? She's your friend?" He shook his head.

"We're more like sisters."

"So how do I become Timmy's father?"

It was back to that. "You have dinner with us." It had been easy enough to cook for three the other night. "Then you spend a little time with Timmy and help me put him to bed before you go back over to Maude's."

"And when Ralph comes over?"

Ralph could be a problem. "We face that when it happens."

David slid off his stool, wiped the cookie crumbs from his mouth and walked toward her. "It's going to happen." He touched the side of her face, brushing his fingertips over her cheek. "If I were him, I'd be planted on your doorstep, ready to take on all comers."

"Sure you would." She tried to laugh, but it sounded stilted.

"I would," he said softly.

Before she realized what he was doing, he lowered his head and brushed his lips across hers. Then he stepped back. "Thanks for finding me a job."

Too amazed to move, Kari simply stared at him. With the briefest of nods, he walked away, letting himself out of her house and leaving her totally dazed.

Chapter Six

That afternoon David called his folks and let them know where he was and what he was doing. Their conversation was short. He'd known they would support him in whatever decision he made. He also called the lawyer he'd talked to in Traverse City. He might have promised to stay until Gail returned, but that didn't mean he was delaying custody proceedings.

The rest of the evening he spent wondering what had prompted him to kiss Kari. It had been an impulsive move. One moment he'd had his hand on her cheek, the next his lips had touched hers.

It was amazing she hadn't slapped his face.

He almost wished she had.

Kissing Kari was ridiculous. Number one, she was keeping his son from him. Number two, she already had a boyfriend. And number three, and most important, he didn't want to be attracted to her. She was Gail's best friend.

Not that he could understand why. Gail had put Kari in a tenuous position. She'd not only left her to deal with an energetic four-year-old, she was asking her to deal with him.

Perhaps what frustrated David most was Kari was dealing with him quite well. So far he'd agreed to do everything she'd asked. He was staying in Michigan instead of heading back to California, living next door to his son not in the same house and waiting for his ex-wife to return from Paris.

Kari Carmichael had to be a magician to have pulled all that off, or a sorcerer who'd woven a spell over him, fogging his mind and arousing his desires. Why else had he kissed her?

Other than he'd found her attractive from the day he first met her, and he liked her concern for his son. She was nothing like Gail, nothing like the women he had dated before Gail, yet he found her smiles enticing and her laughter addictive.

Settling himself on Maude's couch and snapping on the television, he gave up analyzing his feelings. Understandable or not and reasonable or not, he liked Kari Carmichael.

Saturday morning Kari invited David over to have pancakes with his son. She wasn't sure what to say to him, not after that kiss, but Timmy solved her problem. All through breakfast he asked David questions.

Sitting and listening to the two exchange information about why leaves turned color and fell, why birds flew south and why people wore coats instead of growing fur, Kari knew it wasn't going to be long before father and son were best of friends.

She found it difficult to realize only a week before she'd believed the man was dead. She would never forget the day she opened her door and saw him standing on the other side...or that night. She could still remember how his body had felt pressed against hers and the crazy thoughts that had played through her head. She would never understand her reaction.

She couldn't understand her reaction every time she saw David. The moment he'd walked into her kitchen that morning, she'd felt the quivery sensation in her stomach. And whenever he looked her way and smiled, her heart skipped a beat. She was sure of it.

The man looked too good for this early in the morning, his hair neatly combed and his face clean-shaven. He was wearing a gray knit sweater over a white shirt and a pair of jeans that looked brand-new. From the fine blond hairs on the backs of his hands to the scent of his after-shave, he was driving her crazy. She wanted to keep her emotions out of the situation, but her emotions were refusing to listen.

"Wanna help me feed the ducks?" Timmy asked when he was finished with breakfast.

David looked her way, his smile making it all the way to the blue of his eyes and causing her heart to skip another beat. Then he nodded at Timmy. "Sounds like fun."

Timmy hurried to put on his jacket and get the feed. In a moment he was outside. David dallied, looking her way. "What brought on this sudden change in him?"

Kari leaned back in her chair, cradling her mug of coffee in her hands. "We had a little talk last night. I assured him you were no monster and you weren't going to take him away."

"Someday I will," David said seriously.

She was beginning to believe he would. "But not until after Gail gets back, right?"

A half smile touched his mouth. "Right."

He pulled on his jacket and opened the door, but before he stepped out, he said, "Thanks."

As Kari cleaned up the dishes, she watched the two of them toss out the corn. Eagerly the colorful mallards and drab hens scrambled after the corn, and she pictured a children's book with a father and son feeding birds. Many, many birds...of all sizes and colors. Birds in the air, in the trees and on the ground.

Setting the dirty plates in the sink, she went to find her sketchbook and pencil.

Timmy came in a short while later, tossing the empty can in the feed bag and pulling off his gloves and jacket. David didn't follow him in. "He said he had to make some phone calls," Timmy said matter-of-factly. "He'll be over later."

"Oh, he will, will he?" She glanced down at the drawing she'd been working on and wondered what David would think about her drawing him.

"I'm gonna watch television," Timmy said and headed for the living room.

Kari set aside the drawing. What she needed to do was finish the dishes and get to work on the illustrations that were due in two months.

Ten minutes later, the dishes done, she headed for her studio. She'd given the foliage in the picture she was working on a wash of green the day before and was ready to begin bringing out the details of the leaves. What she needed first was a new tube of viridian.

Her tubes of paint were stacked on the top shelf of the closet. With Timmy around, up high and far out of his reach had seemed the safest place to store everything. The problem was, everything was also out of her reach. On tiptoes, she stretched for the tubes on top of a box of charcoal.

"Aunt Kari, can I have a piece of candy?" Timmy asked from the living room.

"No," she yelled back, the tube of viridian almost in her grasp.

"Mommy lets me have candy," he answered, and she heard the clink of the glass candy dish she'd placed high on her bookshelf.

"Timothy Patrick!" Kari yelled, turning toward the door.

The downward movement of her hand caught the edge of the charcoal box, tipping it off-balance and starting the paints on top sliding. Suddenly there was a shower of paint tubes and charcoal raining over her head.

She tried to avoid being hit by either, but she could feel the charcoal dust hit her eyes. Without thinking, she wiped a hand across her lids. A shot of pain in her right eye told her she had trouble.

Keeping that eye closed, she stumbled for the door.

"Just one," Timmy begged from where he stood on the back of the chair he'd pushed up to the bookcase.

"I got something in my eye," she tried to explain and headed for the bathroom off her bedroom.

She splashed water into her eyes, blinking and wiping all traces of charcoal from her face. Her left eye cleared up, but not the right, the burning irritation continuing.

Pulling her lids apart, she tried to see what was in there, but her vision was too blurred. "You okay?" Timmy asked from the bathroom doorway.

She turned toward him, keeping her right eye closed, a mixture of tears and tap water running down her cheeks. "Come here," she ordered and knelt in front of him. "Can you see anything?"

He came over, and she again pulled her lids apart. He looked, then shook his head. "No."

Pain and fear tore through Kari. To lose her sight could be disastrous. "Go next door," she ordered. "Get your daddy. Tell him I need help."

Timmy stood looking at her, not moving. "Now!" she yelled, harsher than she'd intended.

He turned and ran, and she faced the sink again, washing her eyes with water.

David pulled off his sweater and tossed it on the bed. No more impressing people; it was time to get into grubbies. Timmy had said he wished he had somewhere he could climb. Well, that was what he would get. The home-improvement place he'd just called had said they had several kits that would work. A few hours of physical labor and Timmy would have his jungle gym.

David unbuttoned his shirt and pulled it from his jeans. He was about to take it off when he heard a door slam, then Timmy's call. Never had the word "Daddy" sounded so beautiful—or so desperate.

David stepped out of the bedroom to see Timmy in the back room, his blue eyes wide with fear. "Aunt Kari is hurt."

He didn't wait to hear more. Ignoring the fact that he'd taken his shoes off and was half-undressed, he dashed across the grass that separated the two houses. Knowing she never locked her doors, he let himself in.

"Kari," he called out, pausing in her living room.

"I'm in the bathroom," she yelled back. "The one off my bedroom."

David worked his way around the toys on the floor to her bedroom. Through the open door to the bathroom, he saw her leaning over the basin, splashing water on her face. "What happened?" he asked, closing the space between them. "Timmy said you were hurt."

"I got something in my eye. A piece of charcoal, I think."

She turned from the basin, facing him, and held open her eye. "I can't get it."

"Come here with me."

He led her to her bed, sitting her on the edge and positioning himself beside her. "Lean your head back," he ordered, and tilted her face so he could take advantage of the natural light in the room.

He saw something. It was just a tiny fleck of black on her eyeball. "Do you have any cotton applicators?"

"In the bathroom." She motioned toward the room. "Under the sink."

He got one and moistened it, then came back to the bed. "Okay, lie back on the bed."

She did as ordered, and he leaned over her, gently pulling her upper eyelid back. Carefully he brushed the moistened cotton applicator over the spot, but his hand was shaking. To his relief, when he removed the applicator, the spot was gone. "I think I got it."

She closed her eyes, and he waited, leaning over her, his shirt falling open on either side of her. For a moment she did nothing, simply breathed in and out, the action lifting her chest is a most seductive way. He knew this wasn't the time to be thinking of sex, but he was finding that every time he was around Kari, she aroused him. Lying on a bed with her wasn't helping.

Finally, she blinked, and blinked again. When she smiled up at him, he knew he'd succeeded. "I think you did it," she said with a sigh.

"Is she going to be all right?" Timmy asked from the doorway.

"I'm fine now," Kari said, continuing to blink. Only a slight burning sensation remained. "Thank you, Timmy. And you."

She stared up at David, the nearness of his face and body disturbing. If she lifted her hand, she would touch the mat of blond hairs on his chest, would feel the warmth of his skin. If she lifted her head—or if he lowered his— their lips would touch.

Gazing at his mouth, she held her breath. Was she right? Was his head closer than just a moment ago?

"I went over all by myself," Timmy said from somewhere near the end of the bed. "I told him you were hurt."

David looked away from her. "You did a good job, son."

"I know how to call 9-1-1," Timmy boasted. "You want me to call 9-1-1?"

"No, don't call 9-1-1," Kari and David said almost in unison, then laughed.

David helped her sit up. He'd nearly kissed her, and that bothered him. He'd spent the evening before convincing himself he could resist the attraction he felt, and spent the night fighting the dreams of her. He didn't want to get involved.

He had to remember that.

"Now there's a cozy scene," a male voice said from the bedroom doorway.

Both David and Kari turned their heads to look at Ralph at the same time. The man's brows were deeply furrowed, his mouth drawn in a tight line. David could imagine how it looked. Here they were on Kari's bed. His shirt was unbuttoned and hanging wide open. He was wearing no shoes. She—

He glanced at Kari. Her cheeks were flushed, and she looked guilty as sin.

Perversely, David smiled and decided he wasn't going to explain a damn thing.

Kari did.

"I got something in my eye, Ralph. A piece of charcoal, I think. Timmy went and got David, and he got it out."

"How noble." Ralph didn't look as though he thought it was noble. In fact, David was certain the man suspected more had been going on.

Kari was the one who moved first, sliding off the bed and walking over to her bathroom. She grabbed a towel from the towel bar and began patting her face. "My eye's feeling better all the time," she said.

She'd made it clear she didn't want Ralph getting the wrong idea, and David could feel the other man's icy glare. With Timmy already out of the room, it was just the three of them, and it was time for him to get out. It wasn't his style to encroach on another man's territory.

"Well, if you're all right," he said. "I'll be leaving."

"You do that," Ralph said, his tone frigid.

David stopped midway between Kari and Ralph and looked back at Kari. "By the way, do you mind if I build something in your backyard for Timmy to climb on?"

"Something?"

"A jungle gym. You know, one of those wooden things with rope netting and tires to climb on and through. Nothing too elaborate. He was saying he didn't have anything to climb on."

"I guess it would be all right," she said, and he had a feeling she was more interested in his leaving than in what he might build.

"Good." He nodded. "Then I leave you in able hands."

He heard Kari say "Thanks," but he didn't look back. He didn't want to catch her in an embrace with Ralph. To be jealous, he knew, was foolish. Ridiculous.

In the living room, he paused. Timmy was sitting in front of the television, a cartoon on the screen. He seemed more engrossed in smashing two trucks together. "Thanks, guy," David said. "By the way, you want to help me build something this afternoon?"

"Whatcha gonna build?" Timmy asked, putting down the trucks.

"A surprise."

"Really? A surprise for me?"

"Might be." David glanced at his watch. "See you in about an hour."

* * *

"What is going on between you two?" Ralph demanded.

"What do you mean, what's going on?" Kari tossed the towel back into the bathroom. "I told you. I got something in my eye and David helped me get it out."

"That's not what was going on when I found you. The two of you looked pretty damned cozy."

"I was still shaken," she said, but she knew it had been more.

"And what's your excuse for setting him up so he's living next door to you?"

She was surprised by Ralph's undisguised jealousy. "I don't need an excuse. David needs to be near his son and Maude won't be back until May. It worked out best for both of them."

"Don't you mean for both of you?"

"Ralph, you sound like a jealous lover," Kari said, not liking his tone.

"Well, maybe I am. Maybe I'm not wild about some stranger coming into town and taking up with my woman."

"Your woman?"

"Are you saying you're not?"

"I'm saying this is news to me."

"We've been going out for ten months."

"Casual dates."

"I don't have a lot of time."

"You're getting upset over nothing," she assured him. "What David wants is his son. I'm more of a hindrance, a thorn in his side."

"He wasn't looking at you as though you were a hindrance or a thorn."

Kari remembered the moment she'd thought David might kiss her—about the kiss the day before—then she shook her head. "You're reading too much into a look."

Ralph studied her face then turned away. "Whatever you say," he mumbled. "Do you have any coffee?"

Kari couldn't tell what David bought, other than what she could see through her studio window. He dragged the boards into her backyard just before noon, and Timmy was out "to help" in a second. Ralph was loading a program on to her computer, and she decided it wouldn't be a good idea to leave him to go talk to David.

She did have trouble getting Timmy to come in for lunch and finally compromised by letting him take his sandwich outside. Ralph stared out her kitchen window, and Kari knew if looks could kill, David would be dead.

She decided calling Timmy in for a "rest" was a losing proposition. Father and son were still working, Timmy hammering away at a nail in a board, David bolting together boards. If it was a jungle gym, she couldn't tell. When Ralph asked her to walk him to his car, she slipped on her jacket and went with him.

He said nothing until the reached his car, then he faced her. "I think we should get engaged."

"Get what?" Considering his mood all day, a proposal of marriage was the last thing she'd expected...if this was a proposal.

"I think we should get engaged," he repeated, taking her hands in his. "We can go look for a ring this week. This afternoon if you'd like."

It was too sudden. "This is because of David, isn't it?"

"I think it would be a good idea if he knows you belong to me."

"Belong?" The word made her cringe.

He shrugged. "That you aren't available."

It wasn't the way she'd imagined a proposal of marriage. Ralph hadn't mentioned the word love. There'd been no bells ringing. No fireworks. No quivering in the pit of her stomach. Not once in the ten months she'd known him had he left her breathless.

They'd had good times together, and there were a lot of positive things she could say about Ralph Schneider. He was smart, helpful and a hard worker. Steadfast, as Gail had pointed out. He would probably make a good living in his lifetime. All qualities her father considered extremely important. Qualities she should consider important.

There was just one problem. "It wouldn't work."

He frowned. "Why not?"

The answer was simple. "I don't love you."

He looked so stunned, she hurried to finish. "I like you as a friend. I really enjoy going out with you. But I don't love you, and you deserve a wife who is head over heels madly in love with you."

Ralph looked toward Maude's house. "It's him, isn't it? He's got you thinking crazy." He stepped back, breaking contact with her. A shake of his head expressed his disgust. "You're a fool if you think he's serious. What he's looking for is a quick roll in the sack. It will be the same as that guy you told me about, the one who led you on in college then dumped you."

"It's not the same," she argued, determined never to be that gullible again. "David's here to get custody of his son. That's all he wants."

"If that's what you think, then you truly are a fool."

Ralph turned and got into his car. He started his engine and his window rolled down. "I'll give you a week. If you change your mind, give me a call."

She didn't answer and the window went back up. She watched him drive out of her yard. She knew she should feel bad about what had happened, instead, she walked around to the back of her house feeling strangely liberated.

David stood next to a twisted assembly of posts and boards, ropes and tires, studying a sheet of instructions. The ducks watched from the bank of the creek and two seagulls swooped overhead. Otherwise, he was alone. "Where's Timmy?" she asked as she neared.

He glanced her way, then toward her house. "He gave up on me and went in for a nap."

"On his own?" She'd have to see that to believe it.

David nodded. "I think the cold and wind got to him. I checked. He's lying down."

"No kidding." She glanced at the diagram David held in his hands, then down at the pile of boards. The two only vaguely resembled each other. Once again her mind began to create a drawing. "You're giving me all kinds of ideas."

"Oh yeah?" His eyebrows went up and he faced her.

"For a book, a children's picture book," she quickly explained. "Actually, I got the idea this morning when you and Timmy were feeding the ducks. I think I'll call it something like *With My Daddy.*" Kari used her hands to give him a picture. "One page would be 'With my daddy, I feed the birds.' And another would be, 'With my daddy, I build things.'' And I would have a structure that took up the entire page, each board a different shape or size or texture or color, no rhyme or reason to their construction."

David looked down at the wood by his feet. "Are you saying there's no rhyme or reason to this?"

"Is there?" If there was, she certainly didn't see it.

"Ah, ye of limited vision." He grinned and let the diagram drop to the ground. "Boyfriend gone?"

"All gone," she said, the words holding a double meaning.

"You got everything straightened out?"

"Completely." She looked away from David. "He asked me to marry him."

"Congratulations."

Still not looking at him, she went on. "I turned him down."

For a moment, there was silence, the only sounds the quacking of a duck and the wind whistling through the tree tops. Then she heard David sigh. "Because of me?"

The answer was yes, but only in a convoluted way. She looked back at him. "Because I realized I didn't love him. I like Ralph. Like him very much. But—"

"My life's too complicated right now," David said, the concern in his eyes touching her. "You're a—"

He didn't finish, but she knew what he was going to say. She'd heard it before. That she was a very nice person, sweet and shy, but—

There was always that *but*.

"I understand," she said. "Except really this has nothing to do with you." At least not in a realistic way. "It has to do with deciding what I want in a relationship."

"And what do you want?"

She looked up into eyes as blue as a summer day and felt something warm and fuzzy happening inside of her. She knew what she wanted. That sense of being totally alive and on the edge, that wonderful jittery, breathless sensation that came over her every time he was near. "More than Ralph could give me," she said honestly.

"You'll find him," David said softly and touched the side of her face. The electricity raced through her. "One of these days..."

She held her breath, drawn by his gaze. How aristocratic the shape of his nose was, how beautiful the form of his mouth. She watched his lips near and reached out to touch his arms. If she meant to stop him, the action was never fulfilled. The moment his mouth touched hers, all thoughts but one vanished.

Her fingers curled into his jacket to give her stability. Silky nylon and a thick sweatshirt kept her from his body, yet she felt his strength and his need. His tongue invaded, pillaging her soul, and she surrendered, giving willingly. Reason was gone, leaving only feelings.

"Oh, Kari," he groaned over her mouth, the warmth of his breath stoking the fires within. "This isn't the time for me to get involved with anyone."

"I understand," she agreed, then sighed when his lips once again touched hers. The smell of clean honest sweat was an aphrodisiac to her, and she inhaled deeply.

What he was doing, David realized, was crazy, but he couldn't stop. He kissed her mouth, her cheeks and her forehead, nibbled on her earlobe and neck, then blew into her ear. She shivered in his arms, the quick intake of her breath exciting him more. Her hands gripped his arms, her fingers seductively kneading. He pressed his body against hers, jackets and sweatshirts creating a barrier he wanted removed. He longed to touch her naked skin, to know every dip and curve of her body.

The fire within him drove him on, long-denied needs pushing him beyond sanity. He found the zipper of her jacket and pulled it down, seeking the softness of her breasts. The wind and cold didn't matter, no more than the ducks gathering around their feet, clamoring for more food. Nothing mattered until he felt her hand on his, stopping him, and heard her breathless words.

"Don't," she said. "We've got to stop."

He wanted to argue, to ignore her plea. He wanted to bury himself in her softness and know the pleasure she could bring. Nevertheless, he stopped. Letting his hand drop away from her breasts, he looked at her.

"You're right," she said shakily, her eyes glazed with passion. "It wouldn't work."

He didn't want to be right; he wanted to make love with her. "I need you," he confessed.

"Need isn't enough." Not for her. Kari·took a step back, praying her legs wouldn't crumple beneath her. Her knees were shaking, her mind whirling.

"I..." he began, then stopped. She watched him close his eyes and could feel him regaining control. When he looked at her again, the intensity was gone, his expression more resigned. "I'm not going to offer an apology."

She managed a smile. "I wouldn't want one."

Chapter Seven

Kari started for her house. "Wait," David called after her and she hesitated, looking back.

"I want you to know I do appreciate what you're doing ... taking care of Timmy, helping me."

"Being disloyal to my best friend."

"Disloyal?" He closed the gap between them. "What do you mean?"

Letting Gail's ex-husband kiss and touch her was probably her prime sin, but Kari didn't want to think about that. "I should be fighting you every inch of the way, doing everything in my power to keep you from Timmy."

David shook his head. "No, you shouldn't, and do you know why you aren't?"

She didn't have the foggiest idea, other than every time she gazed into David's blue eyes, all sensibility fled. "Tell me why not."

"Because you know what Gail did was wrong, that Timmy should be with me."

Kari looked away from his eyes at the grass by her feet. "I don't know that at all. I know her mother needed her, that's why she came back here. And that Timmy loves her."

"And that she lies."

Again, she glanced up. "I'll help you reestablish a relationship with your son, but don't ask for more. I've known Gail for twenty-three years. We started kindergarten together. We've been through thick and thin. Been like sisters. I've known you barely a week."

"I wonder if she would be as loyal?"

Kari didn't know the answer. It didn't matter. "I'll see you later, okay? I'm going to work on my paintings."

He merely nodded, and she went inside.

Kari tried to concentrate on the painting she was working on, but she kept glancing out the studio window. David had gone back to work on the jungle gym. He'd taken off his jacket and pushed the sleeves of his sweatshirt up to his elbows. The wind blew his hair about and pressed his sweatshirt against the hard lines of his chest.

Soon she was sketching him as he bolted, then unbolted boards together. She tried to capture on paper the concentration and frustration that showed on his face. When he walked away, leaving her without a model, she waited for his return. It wasn't until she heard his car pull out of the drive that she put down her sketch pad and returned to her painting.

He came back about a half hour after Timmy got up and while she was starting dinner. He stacked the boards in a pile, along with the ropes and tires, picked up his tools, then walked toward her back door.

"Come on in," Kari yelled when he knocked.

"Is it done?" Timmy asked, racing in from the living room and making a beeline for the back door.

David stopped him. "No, it's not done. I'm afraid there's going to be a delay." He looked her way. "The reason I can't put it together is they left out a complete section, and, of course, it was the last set like this that they had in stock. They've ordered another, but it will be mid-week before it's delivered. Sorry, guy." He knelt in front of Timmy. "I really thought I could have it up for you to-day."

"That's okay." Timmy turned away and slowly started back to the living room, his little shoulders slumped.

"The weather's supposed to be nice tomorrow. Mid-seventies," David said, straightening to his full height. "How would you like to go to Lake Michigan?"

Timmy stopped and looked back, then over at Kari. "Her, too?"

"Of course."

David smiled her way, and she immediately felt the quivering in her stomach. It was ridiculous, but she couldn't seem to control it. What she could control was how much contact she had with the man. "I don't think so."

"You're welcome, you know," he said sincerely.

She groped for an excuse. "I—I have a lot of work to do. Those paintings—"

"Then I can't go," Timmy said seriously.

"Sure you can," David insisted. "We don't need her along. We can have fun. Have you been to Lake Michigan before?"

"I don't know." Timmy moved closer to Kari. "I just know I can't go."

He looked scared, his thumb going to his mouth, and that bothered Kari. As far as she knew, while tending her mother, Gail hadn't had time to take Timmy anywhere except to the store, and over to Kari's house when things got too depressing for Gail to stand. And once Gail's mother was dead and buried, Gail had immediately started looking for a job. There hadn't been money for sight-seeing. "I don't think he has," she said.

"That means it would be a new adventure for both of us," David said enthusiastically. "Just you and me embarking for lost horizons."

The enthusiasm didn't help. Timmy clung to her legs, a wary look in his eyes, and David looked at her. "I guess we won't be going unless you come along," he said. "Could you, please? We can keep it short. Maybe a couple of hours. It's not that far to the lake, is it? The way the clerk at the home-improvement store talked, it's only a few miles away. I'll buy some subs and cans of soda. We can have a picnic."

"Please," Timmy echoed from her side.

She knew then that he really wanted to go, that it was fear holding him back, the same fear that they were trying to overcome. To say no would deny David and Timmy a chance to bond. Reluctantly, she smiled and shook her head. "How am I supposed to hold my ground when the two of you gang up on me? Okay, but only for a couple of hours. I really do need to work on those paintings."

"I'll help," Timmy offered.

"Oh, no...no, no, no." She half laughed, and David had a feeling there was more to the story. She explained. "Timmy helped me one day when Gail was still around. Thank goodness it was just a sketch he decided to color. Now he knows where his paper and colors are."

"I can draw real good. You want to see?" Timmy asked.

David looked at Kari and caught her slight nod, then looked down at Timmy. "I sure do. Draw me a picture. Okay?"

"Okay." Grinning, Timmy ran from the room.

Later that night, David looked at the picture Timmy had drawn. Four circle people with stick arms and legs filled the page. Timmy had identified each.

"That's me," he'd said, pointing to the smallest. "And Mommy." He'd pointed to the tall figure beside him. "And Aunt Kari." He'd placed her away from the figures of his mother and him, but not as far away as the fourth figure.

"And this is?" David had asked, pointing to the fourth figure.

"You." Timmy had looked at him as though it should have been evident.

What was evident, David decided, was he had a ways to go before Timmy accepted him. On the other hand, as Kari had said before he left, at least Timmy had included him in the picture. It was a start.

It was eleven o'clock when David came over the next day. "You two ready?" he called, poking his head in through the back door. "It is absolutely gorgeous out here."

"Ready," Kari said, putting the last glass from the dishwasher on the shelf.

Timmy came running from the living room. "Are we going now?"

"We're going." He looked her way and smiled. "If your Aunt Kari gets a move on it."

"I'm coming, I'm coming." She grabbed a jacket for Timmy and one for herself and patted her back pocket, making sure she had her driver's license, just in case, and some money, also just in case. "Ready when you are."

They took David's car, Kari strapping Timmy in on the passenger side and taking the back for herself. It only seemed right. The trip was to bond father and son. She was only along for Timmy's sake.

And she noticed David didn't object.

Timmy talked the entire drive. "Are there sharks where we're going?" he asked. "Did you know sharks eat people? Have you ever seen a shark? Do bears really sleep on the dunes? Why do seagulls poop when they fly? When will we get there?''

By the time they reached their destination, David had answered Timmy's last question a dozen times. Kari told Timmy he was to stay out of the water and stay close to them, but the moment she released his seat belt, he scrambled out of the car and was off at a run, dashing down the path toward the water.

''Timothy Patrick, don't you dare go into that water,'' she yelled after him, and took off running down the path herself.

David followed to the top of the path, then stopped. Timmy was fast, but Kari was faster. She caught him just before he reached the water. From where he stood, David could hear Timmy laugh when she lifted him off his feet and swung him around in a circle. Kari was also laughing. And then she set Timmy down and gave him a hug. David was pretty sure Timmy was also getting a lecture. When he walked away from her, it wasn't far.

Going back to his car, David got the blanket he'd brought and the cooler of soda pop and sandwiches. The parking area was nearly deserted, only three other cars filling the spaces. The clerk who'd given him directions had told him if he took Esch Road, the beach at the end would be good and not as populated as the ones in Empire or along Sleeping Bear Dunes, especially at this time of the year. It had sounded ideal to David. He was looking for a quiet place to spend time with his son...and with Kari.

With Kari. He pushed his trunk closed. He certainly wasn't *with Kari* today. Oh, she was along, but she wasn't with him. She'd made it clear yesterday where her loyalties lay. Her sitting in the back seat today had made it clear what their relationship was. She was the chaperon, the caretaker.

It irritated and frustrated him.

He knew how she'd responded to his kisses, how warm and giving she'd been. He knew how he'd responded. If she hadn't stopped him, they would have ended up in bed.

"And that would have been wrong," he said, then looked around, hoping no one else had heard him talking to himself.

The timing was wrong, and the situation was wrong, but the feelings weren't wrong. He was convinced of that. It wasn't just hormones or he would have been aroused by the girl in the grocery store that morning. She'd definitely made it clear she was available.

"Damn it all," he muttered and started for the path to the beach. "Why her? Why now?"

Kari saw him coming down the path the same time a wave broke close to the shore, bubbles of frothy foam rolling up onto the smooth golden sand near her feet. She scrambled back, and yelled his way. "Need any help?"

"Where do you want to eat?" he called back.

She looked around. Timmy had run ahead, chasing seagulls, and a young couple and their dog were about half a mile farther down the beach. Two older men strolled toward them, deep in conversation, while back from the water, at the base of a small dune, two women sat on a blanket. A few feet away from them, a boy around Timmy's size was building a sand castle.

David reached her side just when the boy and Timmy saw each other. Timmy veered away from the gulls and the water, and the boy rose from his sand castle.

David started to call after Timmy, but Kari put a hand on his arm. "Let them get acquainted. Timmy doesn't get enough opportunities to be with others his age. We can put your blanket down over there." She pointed to a sheltered spot back from the water and not too far from the two women and boy, yet isolated from them because of a jut in the bank.

David watched the two boys greet each other. Like puppies, they gingerly approached and circled each other, gauging how to respond. And then, with no visible clue of how or why, they'd determined who would be the leader and who would follow and were laughing and talking.

"He needs more interaction with children his age," Kari said. "He needs to be in nursery school."

As if to emphasize her point, Timmy came running up to them, the other boy by his side. "This is my friend Johnny," he said. "And this is my Aunt Kari, only she's not really my aunt. And my daddy, who I thought was dead, but he's come back from heaven. He tried to steal me, and we had to call the cops," he said seriously to Johnny. "And my mommy said not to go anywhere alone with him, but sometimes he's nice. He's trying to build me something to climb on, only he can't because it's not all there."

"Glad to meet you, Johnny," Kari said.

Johnny looked them over, then his attention switched back to Timmy. "Come on, let's play." He started off at a run. "Last one is a dip stick."

"Don't go near the water," Kari yelled after them, but the boys headed inland, scampering up the grass-covered dune she'd suggested they set their blanket near.

"Well, that explains why he wouldn't come alone with me, and at least 'sometimes' I'm nice," David said and started toward the same dune. "I'm going to put this cooler down."

"I'll help." She went with him, helping him spread out the blanket.

A breeze off the lake made the air feel cooler than it had at her house, but the dune offered some shelter. Sitting down on the blanket, she cupped a hand over her eyes, shielding them from the glare of the sun, and gazed out over the water. Far off on the horizon, a steamship inched its way north, probably its last trip before the lakes turned to ice.

"I never realized a lake could be so big," David said, sitting beside her. "You can't see the other side. It's like looking out at the ocean."

"Except the water's not salty." She glanced his way. He was squinting, tiny lines crinkling near his eyes, and his hair was blowing in the wind. "Gail said you had a view of the ocean from your house."

He nodded. "That was a nice place. More expensive than I could afford, which the prosecutor took pride in pointing out, but Gail had wanted it."

"You still have it?"

He looked back out at the water, his expression neither angry nor sad. "The bank repossessed it. Payments are a little difficult to keep up from a jail cell."

"You lost a lot, didn't you?"

His gaze switched to her. "My wife, my son, my self-respect and just about everything I owned."

"It was your partner who did it to you?"

He shrugged. "He's the one who did the embezzling, then framed me. It was my stupidity that did it to me." Wryly, he laughed. "My naive trust that I could believe whatever my best friend told me, that I didn't need to worry. Be careful, Kari. Those best friends will get you."

"Gail's not like that," she said right away, then wondered who was being naive. She wouldn't be in the situation she was in right now if not for Gail.

He didn't argue. He just reached over and brushed the hair blowing across her face back out of her eyes, his fingertips resting along the side of her neck. "I thought about you last night."

"You did?"

David heard the slight catch in her voice, saw the way her eyes searched his face and felt the rapid pulse of her heart through his fingertips. His own heart was racing wildly. "I know it would be foolish to complicate matters by getting involved with you. And I don't want to do anything that might jeopardize my chances of getting custody of Timmy. But..."

She licked her lips, and the sight of her tongue sliding out and over them, moistening them, was more than he could stand. "Oh, Kari."

He kissed her. Not gently but forcefully, his arms going around her and dragging her close. He kissed and touched, and satisfied the need that had been eating at him ever since he'd stopped kissing her. And he reveled in the fact that she didn't push him away, that her mouth was moving with his, that her breathing was as erratic as his and that her hands were roaming over his back.

Together they fell back on the blanket, the sand and rough wool cushioning their bodies. Stretched out, he pulled her hips closer, wanting the contact. "I dreamed of this last night," he whispered near her ear. "Dreamed I made love with you."

"We can't make love," she said, and began to pull back.

"No." He stopped her. "We're not going to make love. Not here. Not now. But someday."

He kept kissing her, absorbing the taste of her, inhaling the scent of her. Like the waves breaking only yards away, a wave of tension broke within him, pouring forth emotions that surged to the surface. Wild and wonderful, he let himself flow with the tide. Each kiss took him deeper, each parry with his tongue exciting his imagination.

He would swear he heard Kari saying, "Excuse me." But he knew that couldn't be, not the way her mouth was playing against his.

"Excuse me!" he heard again, the woman's voice more strident this time. "Mister. Lady."

David felt Kari draw back, and he didn't stop her. They both looked up.

Standing near the edge of the blanket was the younger woman who'd been with Timmy's new friend Johnny. "Have you seen the boys?" she asked.

David could now hear, farther away, the older woman calling for Johnny. "They've disappeared," the woman standing above them said.

"Disappeared?" Kari gasped and pushed herself to a sitting position, brushing her tousled hair aside and straightening her clothes as she looked toward the water.

David stood, his gaze going up the bank behind them, toward the trees that lined the shore. That was the direction in which the boys had been headed.

"I've been calling Johnny," the woman by their side said. "My son usually doesn't go very far away and comes right back. I'm getting really worried."

"Have you checked the woods?" David asked.

"The woods?" She looked in the direction of the trees. "He does love to climb trees."

All three of them scrambled up the grass-covered dune, the older woman staying behind on the beach. Once they reached the higher ground and the edge of the trees, thick underbrush hampered their progress, but they worked their way along the edge of the dunes until Kari spotted a wide path that led into the woods. It was Johnny's mother who found the boy's tracks.

Once again, David shouted Timmy's name. Far off up ahead, he heard a faint response. The cry was definitely a child's.

David kept calling out Timmy's name and shouting for him to stay where he was. Johnny's mother also called out her instructions. Hurrying along the path, they worked their way deeper into the trees. Nevertheless, they nearly missed them.

"Up here," David heard as he neared an old wild cherry tree.

All three of them looked up.

Johnny was among the highest branches, roughly twenty feet up the tree. Timmy was only fifteen feet or so off the ground. He waved down at them, and Kari gasped. David couldn't make a sound. His stomach was in his throat. Heights had always scared him.

"See how high I can climb," Timmy yelled down at them. "Johnny can climb higher, but he's done this millions of times. This is my first time. I'm X-Man. I can climb anything."

"Johnny Lindstrom, you come down here this minute," his mother ordered, her face an ashen white.

David could see that Timmy had to come down first if Johnny was going to get down. That or Johnny would have to climb over Timmy. Not exactly a safe situation for either boy. "Timmy, you're going to have to come down first," he instructed.

For a moment, he thought everything was going to be fine. Timmy moved a little, looked down, then reached down with one foot. But then, the foot went back to where it had been and Timmy yelled, "I can't."

"You're a scaredy-cat," Johnny yelled from above. He'd already come down one branch.

"I can't," Timmy repeated, and David heard the hysteria setting in.

"You can do it," he encouraged. "Just put your foot down until you touch the next limb."

"I can't," Timmy cried, not moving.

"I'm gonna climb right on over you," Johnny taunted from high above, coming down another limb.

"No!" Kari and David yelled at the same time, then looked at each other.

"I've got to go up," David said.

Kari knew from the ashen pallor of his face that it wasn't an idea he relished. "I'll go," she offered.

"No, he's my son."

She heard him take a deep breath and watched him rub his hands along the sides of his jeans. The third time he looked up the tree, then breathed deeply again, she wondered if he would go. And then he grabbed a branch and began.

Every foot he rose from the ground, her stomach twisted tighter. "You stay where you are, Johnny," David ordered as he climbed, and Johnny's mother repeated the command.

To Kari's relief, Johnny stayed where he was... and Timmy hung on.

Kari wasn't sure how David was going to get Timmy down once he did reach him, and she had a feeling he didn't know, either. When he was just below Timmy, the boy within grasp, David stopped. She couldn't clearly hear what he was saying, but she could tell he was asking Timmy to move his leg. She hadn't realized she'd been holding her breath until Timmy did move his leg. Then she sighed in relief. And when Timmy moved a hand, she again sighed.

She was all out of sighs when both of David's feet touched the ground and he swung Timmy out of the tree. Going forward, she hugged Timmy, then began lecturing him. "You took ten years off of my life."

Her gaze met David's. "Both of you."

"Took ten years off mine." He rubbed his hands along the sides of his jeans and looked up the tree. Johnny was only a few feet from the ground. Reaching over, he helped him out, too, and set him down in front of his mother.

Johnny got a swat and a lecture all the way back to the beach. His mother didn't even thank them for their help, and Kari was sure she blamed them. Both women and Johnny left, walking off toward the parking area, and Kari knew Timmy had lost his friend for the afternoon. "Ready for a submarine sandwich and a soda?" she asked Timmy.

"Sure," he said and plopped dejectedly down on the blanket.

"I need a drink," David said, sinking down beside his son. "A stiff drink."

"Sorry," she said, digging through the contents in the cooler. "Unless you have something like that in here under a soda label, I can't help you."

"I was scared," Timmy said from where he sat, his head down. "Johnny wasn't, but I was."

"I was scared," David admitted, putting an arm around his son's shoulders. "There's nothing wrong with being scared. But sometimes you just have to work your way through being scared."

"Like I did?" Timmy's head came up and he looked at his father.

"Just like you did. You did a great job."

"I did, didn't I?" He looked at her. "Did you see me, Aunt Kari?"

"I saw you. You did a great job."

"I wanna big sandwich and a cola," he ordered.

When they were finished eating, Timmy ran down to the water to toss stones. He asked David to join him, and David said he would, "In a minute."

David waited until Timmy was out of hearing range. "I was terrified," he said to her.

Kari touched his hand. "I could tell."

"I thought he was going to fall and I would lose him." He kept his gaze on Timmy. "I don't want to lose him, Kari. I should have been paying attention to where he was, what he was doing. Instead—"

She knew what he'd been doing...what they'd been doing.

"I know we're going to be seeing a lot of each other until Gail returns," he said. "To be honest, as much as I'd like to have Timmy living with me, as long as I have to work, it's better if he stays with you."

"Oh, thanks."

Glancing her way, he half smiled. "You're the one who made the rules."

"No, Gail seems to be setting the rules."

"Until she gets back," he said, "you and I need to work out an arrangement that's in Timmy's best interest."

"Nursery school?" she asked, feeling that was in Timmy's best interest.

"If you think he needs it, then I'll pay for it."

That was more than Gail would probably have offered. "He needs it."

"Then we'll get him in nursery school. What I was thinking of, however, is you and me. What if I promise to keep my hands off you, and if I forget that promise, you slap my hands?"

The thought of his hands on her warmed her from the inside out. "And if I can't keep my hands off you?"

He smiled and leaned close, his lips brushing across hers. Then he rose to his feet. "I'll slap your hands."

Striding down to the beach, he joined his son. Kari sat where she was, staring at the two of them. There could be a lot of hand slapping going on in the next two months.

Chapter Eight

When Kari looked back over the month of October, she realized there had been no hand slapping. Perhaps because they both got so busy. They signed Timmy up for nursery school that next week, and three mornings a week he joined ten other children his age. That gave him a chance to socialize and Kari time to work on her illustrations. By the end of the month, she had six of the ten paintings finished and the idea for her own book was developing.

Timmy had come up with the title. She'd been trying to decide what to fix for dinner one night when he'd come into the kitchen. "When Daddy comes home," he'd said, "we're gonna carve pumpkins."

That night, after Timmy had gone to bed and David had left, Kari had sat sketching the three pumpkins they'd carved, and she'd known she had another drawing for *When Daddy Comes Home*. Father and son would be carving their pumpkins, while all around them would be dozens of jack-o'-lanterns of all sizes and shapes, expressions and designs. The sketch went into her folder.

While she'd been sketching and painting, David had been working at the resort. He'd said he found his job interesting and that Wayne Peterson was very helpful, explaining the software the resort used and the accounts they had set up. "Not that I feel like a whiz with this electronic transferring of funds," David had told her. "But it's the wave of the future."

Ralph had been telling her the same thing. He'd said in another ten years checkbooks would be obsolete, and that bothered her. Not that she wanted to hold back the future, but at least with a check you or the bank had a receipt of payment. That had helped her once when a company claimed she hadn't paid for an order. She'd sent a copy of the canceled check and the matter was resolved.

Kari didn't always understand what David was telling her about his job, but that was because she'd never been that interested in business matters, an attitude that had really upset her father. With him she'd found it easiest to simply nod and seem to listen. With David, she really cared. His enthusiasm was catching.

One week before the end of the month, after dinner, he leaned back in his chair and patted his stomach. "Good meal. If I keep eating like this, I'm going to gain twenty pounds."

"More coffee?" she asked, pleased with the compliment. After cooking for one for so long, she was enjoying fixing meals for three.

"Please." He leaned forward again, pushing his cup toward her. "Can I tell you about what happened today? It was really weird . . . actually scary."

"Scary?" she asked, grabbing the coffeepot from the counter.

He nodded. "I went into the capital assets' file, and I was off ten thousand dollars. I couldn't figure it out. I'd run a balance on it just last night, hadn't done a thing that should have changed the final figures, but there it was—or rather, wasn't. I was ten thousand short.''

She could understand his concern. A man once accused of and locked up for embezzlement wouldn't want any money missing.

''Thank goodness Wayne's such a wizard with computers,'' David went on. ''I showed him what was up, and he went into the system, found the problem and corrected it in a minute.''

''That's good.'' Kari poured more coffee for both of them. ''Your blood pressure back to normal yet?''

''Barely. All I could think was, here we go again. I was really concerned because I know a lot of people are watching me right now. I may have been cleared of embezzlement, but there are still some who question why I didn't know what was going on.''

''You mean Wilkerson?''

''Wilkerson. Those deputies. People around here.''

''People around here treat you with suspicion because you're an outsider.'' She put the coffeepot back on the counter. ''That's just the way it is around Bear Lake and in a lot of areas in northern Michigan. If you haven't lived here year-round at least twenty years, you're an outsider and will be treated with suspicion. Have you ever noticed how most of the natives don't use turn signals? In their opinion, if you're from around here, you know where they're going, and if you're not from around here, it's none of your business.''

Sometimes David found the close-knit attitude of the community frustrating. Other times he liked it. After living all of his life around L.A., where neighbors rarely knew each other's names much less what anyone was doing, northern Michigan was a step back to another time. At Bear Lake, everyone knew what you were doing.

Or what people had done in the past.

He was learning about his ex-wife, about her alcoholic mother, about the poverty Gail had known and the dreams she'd had. He didn't condone her lies, but he was beginning to understand what had prompted them. Gail had wanted to escape her past, so she'd made up a new past. For a moment in time, he'd fulfilled her dream, and then he'd let her down.

He hadn't forgiven her for lying to him and taking Timmy, but the anger wasn't as intense. They'd even had two halfway civil conversations in the past week.

"The Halloween party next week will help people get to know you," Kari said and grinned. "Soon you'll be just like the others, coming over here and telling me all the local gossip."

"I don't think so." He glanced toward the bathroom where Timmy had gone to wash his hands. Though he doubted the boy could hear him, he lowered his voice. "Once I have legal custody of him, we're gone."

Kari tried not to let the idea of never seeing the two of them again bother her. David had been up-front from the beginning. He was here for his son. His prime purpose for coming over to her house every night and every weekend wasn't to see her. Those few kisses and the fact that he sometimes stayed to talk to her after Timmy had gone to bed meant nothing. It would be ridiculous for her to take it too seriously.

Oh sure, he'd said he wanted to make love with her, but sex, she knew, wasn't love. She'd learned that the hard way while in college.

She just wished she didn't get such a warm feeling whenever David smiled at her, didn't feel like crowing when he praised her cooking, or didn't dream of him every night.

Just thinking about those dreams gave her a warm feeling, and she concentrated on her coffee.

Timmy came out of the bathroom, his hands still dripping. "All clean," he said, showing them his fingers and palms. "I'm ready to play Candyland."

"You go get the board set up," David said and lifted his mug. "I want to finish this."

He waited until Timmy had left the kitchen before turning to Kari. "I got that camouflage material you wanted. It's in the back of my car. You sure you want to take the time to make a costume for him? I could pick up something at the store."

"This is going to be special." She could hardly wait to get started. "And what about you? Have you decided on a costume yet?"

David put down his mug and slid back his chair. "I'll think of something."

The night of the community Halloween party, Kari was curious to see what David had thought of for a costume. As they waited for him to come over, Timmy growled and grunted and lumbered around her living room, giving his interpretation of an evil troll.

She was pleased with the way he looked. Appliquéing camouflage onto camouflage and stuffing it had created bumps and warts that changed Timmy's shape so he might have been one of the supernatural forest dwellers of Scandinavian mythology. He didn't look all that different from the trolls she'd been drawing and painting for the past few months.

He wore no mask, but she'd applied makeup to his face and his skin was now a gruesome green in color. Her front door opened, and Timmy jumped down from the end of the couch. "Grrr," he growled, lurching menacingly toward the door. "Grrr."

David stepped into the living room and closed the door behind him, blocking out the wind and cold. He feigned shock at the sight of Timmy, raising his hands in mock defense. "Oh my gosh, it's a monster!"

"No it's not, it's only me, Daddy," Timmy said quickly, standing straighter, his expression concerned.

David leaned closer, as if having to check. "Well, what do you know?"

"I'm a troll. A forest dweller," Timmy eagerly explained. "I scare people."

"You certainly scared me." David looked over at Kari.

Her costume was a complete contrast to Timmy's. She was dressed in white lace and tulle, a white leotard, white tights and white boots and there was glitter in her hair, little stars of silver in a sky of mahogany dark-brown. She was wearing more makeup than usual, her natural beauty enhanced. She was the fairy princess of her paintings—Peter Pan's Tinker Bell in living form—and when she stood, a chorus of tiny bells sounded all around her.

"We'll know where you are tonight," he said softly, unable to draw his gaze away from the pale pink of her lips.

"And what are you?" She frowned, more bells tinkling when she cocked her head to the side.

"What are you, Daddy?" Timmy repeated, pulling at the edge of David's newly purchased ski jacket to open it wider.

"I'm, uh . . ." He couldn't very well say he hadn't come up with a costume. Pulling his gaze away from Kari, he looked down at his son. "I'm a modern-day prince, come to save the fairy princess from the wicked troll."

"Where's your sword?" Timmy asked.

Kari laughed. "A modern-day prince?"

"You need a sword," Timmy persisted.

David looked at Kari. "Hey, modern-day princes dress just like regular men. What they have that's different is a title." And he was in luck there.

He reached into the pocket of his slacks and pulled out a name tag he hadn't used from the meeting he'd attended that morning. *Hello, my name is . . .* it said in its pre-printed form. Below that, someone had typed "David Weeks." He pulled out his pen and quickly added some words above and in front of his name. Sticking it onto the sweater he wore beneath his jacket, he read the name tag out loud and bowed. "His Royal Highness, Prince David Weeks, at your service."

"Cop-out," Kari said, laughing.

"Are you really a royal hind nuts?" Timmy asked.

"Your daddy's nuts, that's what he is," Kari said, still laughing. She glanced at the wool slacks he was wearing. "I have some black tights that I think would fit you. And in that bag of dress-up clothes we got for Timmy, there's a jacket I think would be perfect if I added some gold braid. It wouldn't take me but a minute to tack it on."

Perhaps not, but he wasn't going to find out. "No tights. You don't see Prince Charles running around in tights, do you?"

"Can we go now?" Timmy asked. "I wanna show Jason and Chad I'm a monster. They said they had the best-ever costumes, but mine's a million trillion times better."

"At least a million trillion times better," David agreed.

"Just the jacket then?" Kari persisted.

David looked down at his son. "Are we going to let her sew gold braid on a jacket or are we going to a Halloween party?"

"We're going to a Halloween party," Timmy answered and faced Kari. "We men have decided."

David laughed and gave Timmy a gentle push toward the kitchen. "Okay. Go get your jacket on. We're going, with or without this crazy fairy princess who wants to spend her night sewing."

Timmy ran to the back door for his jacket and David looked at Kari. "Thanks for the offer, but I think you are now seeing the difference between an accountant's mind and a creative mind." Then he smiled. "You look beautiful."

She shook her head, the bells jingling. "And you look handsome as ever, even if you aren't wearing a costume."

"Ah, but I am." He tapped his newly attached name tag.

"I got my coat," Timmy said. "But I can't get it on."

Kari and he looked over at Timmy and started laughing. She'd done a great job of turning him into a monster. His jacket simply wasn't made for monster arms.

The high school gym was used for the annual Halloween party, with children and adults of all ages gathering in the warmth of the building. The smell of hot apple cider with cinnamon greeted Kari the moment she walked through the doors, and laughter and noise bounced off the walls. The blanket they'd wrapped around Timmy was left on one of the bleachers, along with their coats and jackets, and the moment Timmy's friend Chad came over, the two boys were off at a run, each holding a bag for the candy and treats they would get at the various games. Kari and David stayed close behind.

There were games of skill and games of luck, apples to dunk for or catch on a string, pumpkins to decorate with markers and a cakewalk. In one of the classrooms, a haunted house had been set up, and in one corner of the gym a woman dressed like a gypsy sat behind a table with a crystal ball. The sign above her head said, Madame Zarnoff, Fortune-Teller.

"Tell your fortune?" the woman asked as they passed her table.

David glanced Kari's way. "What do you say? Want to find out if there's a tall, dark stranger in your future?"

She glanced up at his blond hair and blue eyes and grinned. "I'm not sure I'm up to meeting any more strangers."

"Then perhaps for you?" Madame Zarnoff asked David, her veil concealing all of her face except for her eyes.

The booths were being run by Bear Lake's Rotary Club members, yet Kari didn't recognize the woman or her voice. "Who are you, anyway?"

"Madame Zarnoff." The woman nodded slightly and indicated the chair on the other side of her table. "Please, sit down."

"Why not?" David said and pulled out the chair. "I'd like to know what the future holds. Lots of money, I hope. And of course, happiness." He smiled up at Kari. "See any tall, dark strangers for me?"

"I see for you..." Madame Zarnoff began, and Kari looked into the crystal ball on the table. All she could see were reflections of the room.

"Perhaps not a stranger." Madame Zarnoff glanced up, and smiled. "And she is not so very tall." She looked back at the crystal ball. "Hmm, and another."

"Probably my ex," David said, somewhat resigned. "She's bound to come back one of these days."

Again Madame Zarnoff smiled. "One will end up in your bedroom and one will work in your office."

David laughed. "Then we're not talking about my ex, because she's not ending up in either of those places."

"I also see a little boy."

Safe bet, Kari decided. Madame Zarnoff had undoubtedly seen them with Timmy.

"No," she corrected herself. "I see two boys and a girl."

"Two boys and a girl. Wow." Grinning, David egged her on. "Are they mine?"

"They are yours," she said seriously.

"Okay, then are these three children from the woman in my bedroom or the woman in my office?"

"I am not sure," Madame Zarnoff said, a question to her tone. Above her veil, her brow was lined with a frown. "What I am seeing is becoming very hazy. You must be careful. Something is clouding your future. Someone you trust."

Kari didn't like the direction things were going in. What had started out as fun was turning too serious. "Come on, David," she urged, wanting to leave.

He didn't move. "This person I trust. Is it one of those two women?"

"No," Madame Zarnoff said solemnly, gazing into his eyes. "It is not a woman. You must be careful. Very, very careful."

The woman's tone sent a chill of dread down Kari's spine and she reached out and touched David's shoulder. She could feel the tension in him.

Leaning back, Madame Zarnoff looked up at her. "And now for you?"

"Whoa," David said, staying in his chair. "If it's not a woman—?"

Madame Zarnoff looked back at him. "There is nothing more I can tell you. Your future is up to you, it's in your hands now."

Kari let out a sigh. What was she thinking, getting all worried? *Your future is up to you. It's in your hands.* Wasn't that true for everyone?

Madame Zarnoff was no fortune-teller. She was simply an ordinary person. Probably a cousin or sister of one of the Rotary Club members. That was why she hadn't recognized her. And the ball she was looking into had no special powers. Madame Zarnoff couldn't tell the future any more than she could. "Come on, David," she said. "Let's go find Timmy."

"Good idea," he said and pushed back his chair. Nevertheless, he hesitated a moment before standing. Solemnly, he nodded at Madame Zarnoff. "Thank you."

"Don't tell me you believed her," Kari said as they walked away. "'Your future is up to you,'" she mocked, imitating Madame Zarnoff's tone. "The woman can't tell the future any more than you or I can."

"Maybe not." He let out a deep breath. "On the other hand, maybe she's right. I've been getting lax, slipping back into my old habits of trusting everyone."

The seriousness of his tone concerned Kari. She stopped and faced him. "David, you can't go around distrusting everyone. You've got to trust some people."

"Some people like you?"

"Yes."

Timmy came running toward them. "I gotta go wee-wee."

"I'll take him," David said and glanced down at Timmy's costume. "How do I get him out of this?"

"Velcro in the back."

Kari watched the two of them head out of the gym to find the bathrooms. She had no idea if David did trust her. Sometimes she wondered if she trusted herself.

She jumped when a paw touched her arm. Turning, she faced a big, brown bear.

Ralph lifted the furry head from his shoulders, wiped the sweat from his brow and pulled his steamy glasses off, wiping them on the fur on his arm before putting them back on. "It's hotter than hell wearing this thing. If they're going to have us in costume, they could at least turn the heat down."

Then his gaze swept the length of her. "But then, I guess you would freeze in that skimpy outfit. I see you and your lover boy are still together."

"He is not my lover boy."

Ralph snorted. "You're still together."

"We brought Timmy." She wasn't in the mood for an argument, and she had a feeling that was exactly what Ralph was looking for.

"He's going to use you and leave you, Kari. I know his kind."

"Whether he leaves or stays doesn't matter because he's not using me. There's nothing going on between us. We have a mutual interest. Timmy. And that's all."

"When's Gail coming back, anyway?"

"First part of December."

"A little over a month. Strange she didn't come back right away."

Upsetting better described the situation, but Kari wasn't about to admit that to Ralph. "She had no choice. She had to stay in Paris."

"We all have choices." He glanced beyond her, toward the gym doors, then smiled and leaned closer. "You still have one you could make."

He kissed her before she knew what was happening, then stepped back. "Give me a call when you wise up."

He placed the bear head back over his own and walked away. A moment later, David came up beside her. "Well, I see you didn't miss me too much."

"That, uh—" she wasn't sure what to say "—wasn't something I expected . . . or asked for."

"Tonight seems to be filled with the unexpected."

She had to agree, but one thing did happen as they expected. Timmy didn't want to leave when they said it was time. Nevertheless, he'd fallen asleep in the car before they'd driven the four miles to her house. David carried his son into his bedroom and helped him undress while Kari washed off most of the green makeup that remained on his face.

Timmy barely stirred when they tucked him in and kissed him good-night. Every movement she made was accompanied by the jingle of bells, but they didn't seem to disturb Timmy. Closing the door behind her, she followed David into the kitchen. There he stopped and faced her.

Grinning, he rubbed a fingertip along the side of her face. "You're turning green, my fairy princess."

Surprised by his touch, she tried to ignore the jump of her heart. The fact that she'd gotten some of Timmy's makeup on her cheek and he'd rubbed it off shouldn't create a quivering sensation in her stomach. Perhaps it was the hot dog she'd eaten at the party.

"Well, I'd better be going," he said, only he didn't move and the way he was looking at her wasn't calming her stomach.

"Did you have a good time?" she asked, her voice sounding a little breathless to her.

His smile was enigmatic. "A strange time."

She knew why. "You're still thinking about that fortune-teller, aren't you?"

"The fortune-teller made me uneasy."

The way he was looking at her was making her uneasy. "Do you think I'm going to do something to keep you from getting custody of Timmy?"

He hesitated a moment, then shook his head. "No." Smiling, he touched her hair.

She held her breath, her gaze locked with his.

The silver stars trapped in her hair glittered under the light, while her eyes asked him questions he didn't dare answer. "You make a very pretty fairy princess," he said softly, certain she'd sprinkled her fairy dust over him this night. His mind wasn't working right.

"Thank you." Her smile was magic. "At least you weren't the only one not in costume."

"Ah, but I was in costume...am in costume," he quickly corrected. "You simply haven't been using your imagination."

He reached to the side and snapped off the light, darkening the house so the only light showing was the night lamp in the bathroom, its glow barely reaching them. "I'm wearing my coat of royal red with its gold and silver braid, the one I always wear to state affairs.''

She ran her hands over the sleeves of his nylon ski jacket. "And are you wearing white tights?''

Her voice was ever so slightly shaky, and he noticed she didn't touch his hips. "You have a thing for men in white tights, don't you?''

"No, I just—''

He leaned closer, silencing her with a kiss, knowing it was foolish, yet unable to stop himself. For more than a month he'd restrained himself. For seven days a week, he'd been in her presence, had dinner with her, helped her with the dishes and talked with her. He'd been this close before, smelled her delicious perfume before, seen her smile and heard her laughter, but all those other times, he'd been able to leave when he felt the urge to kiss her coming on. All those other times, he'd been able to tell himself it was wrong to want her, that he wouldn't be sticking around and it wasn't fair to her. All those other times he hadn't felt the pangs of jealousy.

It had been a shock to step into the gym and see another man kissing her. She could say what she liked about Ralph Schneider meaning nothing, but David knew there'd been something. A woman didn't date a man for ten months if there was nothing.

She curled her fingers into his arms, her lips giving and warm against his. "So nice," he said on a sigh and deepened the kiss, wrapping his arms around her and drawing her closer, tiny bells ringing and the tulle and lace of her costume crinkling against his slacks.

So wrong, his subconscious argued, but he chose to ignore the warning. Right and wrong had no meaning.

From the middle to the sides of her mouth, he tasted her, amazed by how freely she responded. He teased with his tongue, and she parried back, exciting him to want more. And when she took him fully into her mouth, he groaned his satisfaction, an ache in his groin begging for equal satisfaction.

His arm hit the wall behind her first, and he rested her back against it. Freeing his arm, he moved his hands to the sleeves of her leotard. Up and down he ran his fingers and along her sides. From the muscling of her biceps to the spring of her ribs and the curve of her small waist, he investigated her body, the stretchy latex holding no secrets. She was firm and soft, warm and giving.

Kari felt her breasts swelling, the nubs of her nipples pressing hard against the silk of her bra. He brought his fingers teasingly close, and she waited, hoping. Then his hands moved past, leaving her wanting.

Every kiss left her breathless and her heart racing. For so many weeks she'd told herself not to think of him. For so many nights, her dreams had teased her with the forbidden. Reality was so much better.

His kisses were wild and wonderful, sexy and sensuous. From the thrust of his tongue to the nibble of her earlobe, he brought her pleasure and surprise. Slowly he worked his way down the side of her neck, tickling her with the tip of his tongue, then nipping little kisses along her bared shoulder. She wanted to cry and to laugh, to purr and to growl.

"White tights would be very revealing at this moment," he said near her ear, and she understood his meaning.

"White leotards can also be very revealing."

He brushed the palm of his hand across one breast, bringing a small gasp to her lips. Immediately he pulled his hand back. "Did I hurt you?"

"No." What hurt was her need for more.

Gently, he touched her again, caressing the curve of her breast before sliding his hand across her nipple. "Very revealing," he agreed.

One sleeve of her leotard, then the other was slipped off, the material sagging to her waist with the ringing of tiny bells. Her bra went next, dropping to the floor with a whisper. Naked to his touch, she sighed and groaned as his ragged breath heated her skin and her nipple was sucked into the moist warmth of his mouth. She ran her fingers through his hair, and closed her eyes, fantasy and reality flowing together.

A wash of rosy pink colored her world, warmth and happiness and tingling sensations pouring through her. She could float. She could fly. She was a fairy princess and he was her prince.

His mouth found hers again, his hands caressing her breasts. She moaned in pleasure, drugged with the ecstasy of his touch.

His chuckle was throaty, his breathing ragged.

"Let's go to bed," he said, barely moving his lips from hers.

"To bed," she repeated, her mind savoring the idea.

To bed and to sleep. To make the dreams a reality. To soothe the ache deep in her body, to satisfy her need for him.

It was what she wanted, yet when he stepped back, breaking the contact of their bodies, she didn't move. He took her hand and started for her bedroom, but she pulled her hand back. Even in the dark, she could see his confusion. Her thoughts were no clearer.

"What's up?" he asked, coming back to stand in front of her. He traced the side of her face with the tip of a finger.

"I don't think we should," she said, wishing she could.

"I, uh . . ." He took in a deep breath. "I could go down to the drugstore, buy some protection."

"It's more than that." A piece of latex couldn't protect her from her feelings. "I just can't."

Once again, he stepped back, dropping his hand to his side. "In other words, all this was—"

"Wrong," she said, realizing how very wrong it had been. Forgetting her bra, she pushed her arms into the sleeves of her leotard, bells ringing as she pulled the material back up to her shoulders. "I can't be just a one-night stand."

"This doesn't need to be for just one night."

"Then for how long?" she asked, her voice stronger. "Two nights? Three? Maybe until Gail comes back? Until you get custody of Timmy?"

He didn't say anything, and she knew her answer.

"I like you, David." Too much, she knew. "If you like me, you'll leave now."

"Did you sleep with Ralph?" he asked.

"No."

She waited for his next question, but it never came. Without another word, David turned and walked out of the kitchen. She heard him cuss when he stumbled over one of Timmy's toys on the living room floor and she heard her front door open and shut. Then her house was silent.

Chapter Nine

Kari dreaded seeing David the next morning. How could she face him after what they'd done the night before?

She hadn't slept well, a fact she regretted when Timmy woke her at seven with, "I can't find my bag of candy."

Vaguely she remembered David setting the bag on the counter in the kitchen before carrying Timmy to his bed. "Look near the sink," she said groggily.

Timmy bounded out of her bedroom and she closed her eyes, then snapped them open and sat up. All she needed was for him to gorge himself with candy and have a sugar high. The way she was feeling, she wouldn't be able to handle it. And there were his teeth to consider.

In seconds she had her robe and slippers on and was in the kitchen. "Two pieces," she said firmly. "That's all you're to have this morning. Then you can have two more after lunch."

"Two?" He looked up at her from where he sat in the middle of the floor, surrounded by his assortment of candy. "Jason's mommy lets him have all he wants."

"Well, I'm not Jason's mommy."

"And you're not my mommy at all."

"No, I'm not," she said, hurt by the reminder. "But until your mommy gets back, you'll do as I say."

He glared at her, but didn't say anything, just began stuffing his candy back into his bag. She thought about explaining why she didn't want him to have more than two pieces, then decided he wouldn't understand. Turning away, she began making coffee.

She was totally unprepared when she heard the back door open. Turning, she saw Timmy closing the door behind him, his bag of candy in his other hand.

She dashed for the door and jerked it open. "Timothy Weeks!" she yelled after him. "Where do you think you're going?"

He paused and looked back at her, then at the house next door. "To live with my daddy."

The moment she stepped outside, he took off at a run, his bare feet making prints on the frost-covered lawn. She felt the cold through her slippers and the frigid early-morning air through her robe and thin nightgown, but Timmy didn't seem to notice. As quick as a puppy, he dashed for Maude's side door and coatroom. Kari hoped David had locked it.

He hadn't.

Timmy ran into the house, and she decided to follow. If she took time to change, Timmy would feel he'd gotten away with his escape. Then next time, who knew where he would head?

She opened and closed Maude's back door as quietly as she could and tiptoed through the coatroom, looking around for Timmy. As far as she could tell, he wasn't there. Opening the next door, she stepped into the kitchen.

All was quiet throughout the house.

"Timothy Patrick," she whispered.

The refrigerator kicked on, its hum startling her. Facing it, she let out a tense breath, then began looking around. The dining area was easy. One glance told her no one was hiding there. The living room took a little longer; she had to check behind the couch and easy chair. She found a pair of dirty socks but no four-year-old boy.

Two closed doors remained downstairs, one to a bedroom and one to the bathroom. Upstairs, she knew, there were two more bedrooms and a half bath. Standing where she was, Kari tried to discern any sounds.

All she heard was the hum of the refrigerator...and the pounding of her heart.

To leave and forget Timmy was a tempting idea. She could let herself out and pretend she'd never come. David would never know she'd been sneaking around, and in time Timmy would return, probably once he'd eaten his fill of candy. Then she could give him a lecture on the dangers of running off.

She took two steps toward the side door and stopped. Later would not work. She had to find him now.

Slowly she cracked the bathroom door open and peeked inside. The toilet seat was up, and a white shirt lay crumpled on the floor, a damp towel beside it, but there was no little boy.

Which left the bedroom.

The door creaked as she opened it and she stopped, holding her breath. Another noise caught her attention, the sound of crinkling paper. Carefully she pushed, widening the opening, and looked inside.

Sitting near the foot of an old-fashioned double bed was Timmy, his bag of candy between his legs.

The moment she saw him, he giggled. Grabbing his bag of candy, he scrambled up on the end of the bed. Kari could see the outline of David's body. A grunt was the first sound he made, a groan the second.

"Hi, Daddy," Timmy said, crawling over David toward his head. "I've come to live with you. Okay? Please..."

"Timmy—" Kari began, then wished she'd kept quiet.

David sat up and rubbed his eyes in confusion, looking directly at her. The comforter and sheet that had covered him fell down around his hips, and she took in a quick breath. David Weeks wasn't a man who slept in pajamas, at least not in the tops of pajamas. His lean torso and muscular arms were there for her to see, from the lines where his tan ended to the blond hairs that covered his chest and tapered down over a very flat abdomen.

Timmy scrambled closer, pulling the bedding toward him as he moved. David's quick grab of the sheet covering his hips told Kari he didn't sleep in the bottoms of pajamas either.

"What the—" he looked down at his son "—is going on?"

"She's mean, Daddy." Timmy's expression was purely angelic. "She said I had to eat a ton of dog doo-doo before I could have any candy."

"She did, did she?" David looked her way, his gaze traveling slowly down the front of her.

His smile made her look down herself, certain her robe was open. To her relief, her sash was still tied, yet she felt naked.

Timmy went on, warming to his story. "And then she said I had to wash my hands in the toilet, and—"

David stopped him. "I don't think your Aunt Kari said any of those things."

"What I said was he could only have two pieces of candy this morning," she explained, glad to hear him take her side. "That's when he took off for here."

"'Cause it's not fair," Timmy said, pouting. "Jason's mommy lets him have all the candy he wants. My mommy would let me have all I wanted."

"I imagine she would," David agreed. "I'll tell you what." He slipped an arm around Timmy's shoulders, bringing the boy closer. "What do you say we negotiate with your Aunt Kari?"

"Nee go shate?" Timmy cocked his head and pursed his lips as if pondering the idea.

David glanced her way. "What would you say, Aunt Kari, to four pieces of candy?"

She saw the three fingers David held down by the side of the bed and understood. "Well..." She tapped a finger to her lips and pretended to consider the possibility. "I really only wanted him to have two, but..." She looked at Timmy. "What about three?"

"Would three work with you?" David asked Timmy.

"I guess," he agreed and opened his bag, rapidly pulling out three pieces of candy.

"Hey, don't I get one?" David asked, leaning closer to look into Timmy's bag.

"Just one," Timmy said seriously and pulled out a piece in an orange wrapper.

"Obviously one he doesn't like," David said, looking her way.

"Obviously." She grinned and leaned back against the doorway. As easily as Timmy had given in to their negotiations, she had a feeling he'd already had far more than three pieces. Nevertheless, the battle was over, and she had won...in a way.

David kept looking at her, and she remembered the night before. How he'd held her and kissed her. Touched her. A warm sensation filled her, her breasts growing sensitive beneath the nylon of her nightgown and a tingling starting deep between her legs.

"The fortune-teller was right," he said softly. "I do have a woman in my bedroom. I just hadn't pictured it quite like this."

Nor had she.

* * *

They had reached the time for the battle of the willpow-ers, David decided. Kari was testing his, and Timmy was testing hers. David wasn't sure how Kari was doing, but he was faring poorly. Being around her was pure torture. He'd nibbled the forbidden fruit and wanted more. Tell-ing himself the timing was all wrong, that nothing could come of their relationship didn't help. Whenever he was close, he wanted to touch, to feel the velvety softness of her skin and the warmth of her body. He wanted more of her kisses . . . and more than that.

What he did was give her as much time as he could to finish her illustrations. He found it fascinating to watch her work, her touch and her colors so like her—light yet bright, soft while remaining strong. She wove her magic through each painting, bringing life to the trolls and fairies and everything else she worked into her pictures. Colorful butterflies and whimsical mushrooms caught the eye, while ugly trolls hid behind gnarled trees, ready to pop out and scare Tommy Magoo and the fairies frolicking about. Each drawing played out the author's words in an involved picture game, and Timmy loved them.

He loved all of the books Kari had illustrated, and reading one at bedtime became an evening ritual David shared with Timmy. From the familiar *Country Mouse, City Mouse* to the strange and mystical *Land of Nod,* Kari always brought her unique touch to the page.

The second week of November, David was sitting on the edge of Timmy's bed, once again reading *Country Mouse, City Mouse,* when the telephone rang. The second ring was cut off before it was finished, and he knew Kari had picked up the phone in the studio. Glancing at his watch, he noted the time. Eight o'clock.

He tried to concentrate on the story and not think about the identity of the caller. It wasn't any of his business, he told himself. It might even be a wrong number...or someone trying to sell her something.

Or it could be Ralph.

David knew he still called her. She'd told him so. And Ralph had come by the resort one day and made it quite clear that he still considered himself in the game, that he was just biding his time. David had thought about telling her she should go out with Ralph, but somehow he could never say the words.

"Well, guess who that was?" she said, coming to Timmy's door a short while later.

"My mommy?" Timmy asked, the eagerness he'd had two months earlier now lacking.

"No, my mommy...and my daddy. They're coming up to spend Thanksgiving with me."

She didn't sound happy about it, David noticed. "Is it a problem?"

"I hope not." She smiled, but it didn't reach her eyes. "They're flying up two days before and staying until the Thursday after."

"Flying in an airplane?" Timmy asked.

"Yes, in an airplane." She spread her arms and swooped into the room like an airplane, stopping near Timmy's head. "Want to go with me to meet them at the airport?"

"Tomorrow?"

"No, in a week." She held up seven fingers. "Seven days from now."

Timmy also held up his fingers, switching from seven to eight, then back to seven. David was more concerned with space than days. "Where are you going to put them?"

"My room, I guess."

"And what about you?"

"I'll sleep on the couch."

"You could always sleep next door." He grinned. "Don't forget, it's in my future."

"That's not what Madame Zarnoff said," Kari reminded him. "And your future's already past. I've been in your bedroom."

But not where he wanted her, not in his bed, with him—alone.

"Me too," Timmy added, not to be ignored. "I was in your bedroom, too."

The phone rang again. Kari bent and kissed Timmy on the cheek. "Time for you to get to sleep."

She laughed when she looked up and saw David puckered for a kiss. She knew what happened when she kissed him. The man was explosive. Things happened, insanity took over.

Kiss him, and she wouldn't be answering any telephone.

"Probably my mother calling back about something she forgot," Kari said and left the room to grab the phone in the kitchen. The moment she heard Gail's voice, she started to call Timmy, then she stopped herself.

"Oh, Kari," Gail said, a sob carrying across the line.

Kari could hear the desperation. "What's the matter?"

"I'm such a fool."

She'd heard that before. Hopes dashed. Dreams wiped out. "Your boss?"

"He found another woman. He's taking her to the Riviera over Thanksgiving, not me." Again, Gail sobbed. "I have to stay here in this dumpy hotel."

"I thought you said your hotel was posh."

"It's a dump," Gail whined. "This city is a dump. It's old and dirty and no one speaks English."

"But you always said you loved speaking French."

"Not when you have to talk it every day. Think about it." Gail sighed. "I'm going to come home."

"Great." Kari just wished she felt more enthusiastic. Wasn't this what she'd been begging Gail to do?

"Can you send me some money?"

"Money? What about the money you've been making over there?" For the past two months, Gail had been saying she was making so much, she couldn't afford to quit.

"I had to spend it." Quickly, she justified her actions. "It's not easy to keep a man like Vernon interested."

"Not easy at all," Kari agreed, considering Gail hadn't succeeded. "I wish I could help you, but I'm a little tight on cash myself right now. Royalties haven't come in, and I won't get paid for these pictures I'm working on until they're delivered and approved."

"Well, then, is David there?" Gail asked.

"He's in reading a bedtime story to Timmy. Don't you want to talk to your son?"

"No, I need to talk to David."

"Well, he's—" She heard the click of a door and looked over to see David had closed Timmy's.

He smiled her way and gestured that Timmy was asleep.

Reluctantly, she held the phone out to him. "It's Gail."

Kari thought he would object. Instead he continued smiling and took the phone from her. "What's up."

Kari's guess was Gail started crying again. David's tone immediately turned sympathetic. Kari doubted Gail was giving him the same story she'd given her, at least not the part about her boss taking up with another woman. When David really started sounding sympathetic, Kari left the kitchen and went into the living room. There she sank down on her couch.

What was wrong with her, anyway? Here she had Timmy's mother and father talking to each other. She ought to be happy. Two months ago he probably would have told Gail to go to hell.

So why did she wish he would?

Why did she want Gail to stay away, never to come back?

Closing her eyes, Kari faced the truth. Having Timmy around was no hardship. She loved the boy. And having

David around was wonderful. They were family. They'd slipped into a routine that was comfortable and fun and loving.

Loving.

The word screamed at her. She loved Timmy and she loved his father. She could deny it until she was blue in the face, but it wouldn't go away. All her talk about loyalty to her friend had been a bunch of bull. She loved David.

And where was it going to get her?

Maybe into his future, if she was to believe that fortune teller. Hazel McGuire, who ran the local bakery, said as far as she'd heard, Madame Zarnoff was a real fortune-teller.

Your future is up to you was what the woman had said. "So what are you going to do?" Kari asked herself. "Give up or fight?"

She looked down at her sweatshirt and sweatpants. She definitely wasn't dressed for seduction, but that could be changed easily enough.

He wanted her in his bed. She glanced toward her bedroom. They really should stay near Timmy. Certainly he wouldn't complain about sharing her bed. He'd suggested it himself two months ago.

"I talked her into giving two weeks' notice," David said from the kitchen doorway and Kari turned to face him, afraid her expression might betray her thoughts.

"Though I'm not sure the old geezer deserves two weeks the way he's been treating her." He shook his head and sighed. "That wife of mine."

Kari stared at him, dumbfounded by his reference to Gail as his wife. When had he stopped bitterly referring to her as his ex? She couldn't remember, yet she suddenly realized he had. "What exactly did she tell you?" she asked cautiously.

"Probably what she told you."

Kari doubted that. "About not being able to go to the Riviera over Thanksgiving?"

He nodded. "Because he wants her to work on a report."

"And because he's taken up with another woman?"

"The guy must be some playboy."

Kari still wasn't sure Gail had told him the same story she'd told her, but he was clearly buying. Standing, she walked over to him. "Are you sending her the money?"

"I'll send it."

"Sucker."

He lifted an eyebrow. "Where's the loyalty?"

"I don't know." Disappointed, she turned away and headed for her studio. "I think I've lost a lot of things. See yourself out?"

David watched her walk out of the room. Leaning against the doorjamb, he grinned in satisfaction. Sometimes the smartest thing a man could do was play dumb.

Kari's parents arrived the Tuesday before Thanksgiving. She and Timmy went to the airport in Traverse City to pick them up. David met them after he got home from work.

In many ways, Carl and Liz Carmichael reminded him of his own parents. Maybe Carl was a little more domineering than his father, but both men saw financial success as the true measure of a person's value. It didn't take David long to understand why Kari had had problems talking with her father and why she'd had to call in Gail for support.

That night after dinner, while Kari was finishing the dishes, her father started questioning her about her finances. David was in the bathroom with Timmy, watching his son take a bath, but he could clearly overhear the conversation. Carl Carmichael might only want what was best for his daughter, but he truly didn't understand how talented Kari was. Capital gains, high profits and strong assets were his measures of success, not aesthetic value and awards.

When her father argued that there wasn't a lot of money in children's book illustrating, David knew the man was right. Kari had admitted as much. It was the reason she took on odd jobs during the year, creating posters and flyers for the local businesses. Those at least, she'd said, were certain dollars.

"Why don't you just forget the book illustrating and concentrate on the advertising?" her father asked.

David waited for Kari to answer and was surprised when she didn't present her arguments. Certain that Timmy was fine, he stepped out of the bathroom.

Kari stood near the sink, looking down at the pot she was scrubbing. Her father was on the other side of the counter. "I could put in a good word for you with the cherry growers," he said. "If you got the advertising contract, you'd be set. You could get out of this house, find something nicer."

"I'll think about it," she mumbled, still not looking at him.

"I thought you liked this house?" David said, walking over to her side.

She looked up at him, and he was surprised by the look in her eyes. The sparkle was gone, the energy and zest. For the first time since he'd arrived in Michigan, he was seeing the Kari that Gail had described.

The change bothered him, but he knew it wasn't the time to push for the reason. Instead, he switched the subject. Smiling, he looked over at her father. "Kari says you moved your business to Arizona."

In the next hour, he picked up a lot of information about the Carmichaels. Liz was a woman who believed a wife should always stand behind her man, and Carl was a man who liked to dominate the conversation. Even Timmy, when he tried to capture their attention before going to bed, was basically ignored.

David waited until he had Timmy in bed before he got Kari aside. "Excuse yourself for a minute," he insisted. "We need to talk."

"But . . ."

"Don't argue."

She excused herself and he grabbed her jacket, tossing it to her before opening the back door. Together they went out into the dark of night.

"What's the matter?" she asked, shivering as the first blast of cold hit her.

"What's the matter?" He put his hands on her shoulders. "Kari, you're letting your father walk all over you."

She hung her head down. She knew what he was saying was true. Gail always used to tell her the same thing. But what could she do? The man was her father. And what he was saying was true. No matter how many awards she got, illustrating children's books was never going to be a stable income. Each book was a new start. Today maybe she was busy. Tomorrow she could be starving.

"You're not going to say anything?" David asked.

She looked up, barely able to discern his features in the darkness. "What can I say? Basically he's right. I would be better off if I forgot the book illustrating and concentrated on advertising."

"Better off, maybe, but what about what you want to do? What about this book idea you've been telling me about? Your *When Daddy Comes Home?*"

"I have no idea if it's going to sell. And even if it does, we're still talking small potatoes as far as financial security."

"Is that what you want? Financial security?"

Again, she dropped her head down. "No." It had never been as important to her as it was to her father.

"Then tell him."

"I can't. He's my father."

He tipped her chin up and stared at her. "What happened to my fighter?"

When he walked away, toward Maude's house, she felt totally deserted. She knew he was disappointed in her. She was disappointed in herself. He just didn't understand how hard it was for her to argue with her father.

Thanksgiving Day, David was the cook. He'd told Kari she'd cooked enough dinners for him that he owed her one and that it would give her a chance to spend more time with her folks. As it was, he was glad to be busy. It was keeping his mind off his other problems.

The fortune-teller, it seemed, had been right about more than just a woman showing up in his bedroom. His future at the moment was hazy, and he did need to be very careful. What he'd stumbled upon at work Wednesday didn't look good. He just hoped when he checked into it after the holiday, he'd find he was worrying over nothing.

"Everyone ready to do some serious people-stuffing?" he asked, carrying the turkey into Maude's dining room. He pointed a finger at Liz Carmichael. "I tried your recipe."

"For the oyster dressing?"

He nodded. "Tastes pretty good, and Timmy thought so, too. Didn't you?"

Timmy nodded, licking his lips.

"If you made it like Mom does, it will be great," Kari said and helped Timmy with his napkin. "Are we going to say grace?"

"I can do it," Timmy said, waving his hand wildly. Then immediately he bowed his head and put his hands together. "God bless Mommy and Daddy, and Aunt Kari and Grandma Carm and Grandpa Carm and—"

"That sounds a lot like your bedtime prayers," David interrupted.

"—And God bless all this food," Timmy finished and looked up. "Can we eat now?"

"Sounds good to me," Kari's father said and reached for the bowl of mashed potatoes.

Kari helped Timmy, serving him a portion from each dish passed. Timmy shoveled in a spoonful of dressing, then a piece of turkey, then a bite of bread, his cheeks bulging like a chipmunk's. David remembered the last three Thanksgivings he'd celebrated. Institutional dinners served in prison dining halls didn't have the warmth of a family dinner, but he and his fellow inmates had stuffed themselves just as Timmy was doing.

Closing his eyes, he prayed that his next Thanksgiving wouldn't again be in a prison dining hall.

"You know about retirement funds, don't you, David?" Kari's father asked while pouring gravy over his potatoes. "Arizona is full of retired people, and you'd be amazed by how few of them have adequate retirement benefits. They thought social security would take care of them, and now they're finding out it won't. A person needs to start planning early, don't you think?"

David had a feeling he knew where the conversation was headed. So did Kari. "Dad, I'm only twenty-eight."

"You're never too young to think about retirement," her father insisted. "That is, if you have enough money to put something aside."

David watched her stare at her plate, then she looked at him. He could see her take in a deep breath, then she faced her father. "Dad—"

"Timmy, what's the matter?" Kari's mother interrupted.

"My head itches."

David looked at his son.

Timmy was scratching his head and there were red welts on his neck and arms. His face was flushed, and he was breathing with his mouth open.

Kari touched Timmy's forehead with the back of her hand, then looked at them. "He feels hot. Look at his ears."

They were red, and his eyes were getting puffy. "Are you okay?" David got up and knelt beside his son. "Do you feel sick?"

Timmy continued scratching his head. "It won't stop itching, Daddy. And . . . and I feel funny."

David parted Timmy's hair, checking his scalp. "My God, his head is covered with those welts."

"Daddy?" Timmy looked up, his mouth open. Every breath he took sounded labored.

And then his eyes closed and he sagged into David's arms. David looked at Kari. "Call 9-1-1."

Chapter Ten

Kari held her foot to the pedal, pushing the speedometer past the limit. Potholes were ignored and curves were taken at a risk. Time was of the essence.

David had gone with Timmy in the hospital helicopter, and her parents had decided to stay back in Bear Lake. They would take care of the food and clean up. She was to call them the moment she knew something.

All she knew was Timmy had to live.

He'd looked so small and helpless on the gurney, the oxygen mask nearly covering his face. His face and body had been covered with red blotches, his eyes swollen shut by the time the helicopter and paramedics arrived. It was his breathing that had scared her, especially when the paramedic explained what was happening. If Timmy's throat swelled shut, they could lose him.

She pressed her foot harder on the gas pedal, thankful there was little traffic on the highway.

The shot of adrenaline they'd given Timmy had seemed to help; nevertheless, it had scared her when she heard his blood pressure and heart rate. Some people died of bee stings. This was basically the same thing.

Traffic picked up as she neared Traverse City, but she dodged in and out, running yellow lights. Her tires squealed as she swung into the hospital parking lot, and she had her key out of the ignition before her car had rolled to a complete stop. Her coat still open, her hair blowing out wildly from the sides of her face, she ran for the emergency room entrance.

"I'm looking for Timmy Weeks or his father, David Weeks," she breathlessly told the woman at the reception desk. "They came in by helicopter."

The woman motioned down a hall. "Mr. Weeks is in the waiting room."

Kari dashed down the hallway, only slowing to a walk the last few feet before the doorway. She could see David standing in a corner of the room, facing the wall, his shoulders slumped. *Don't let Timmy be dead,* she prayed and took a deep, bracing breath before stepping into the waiting room.

"How's he doing?" she asked, coming up beside David.

He looked at her, and she could see the tears in his eyes. Before he spoke, he, too, took a deep breath. "The doctor says he's holding his own, that the next hour or so will be the telling point."

For a moment he squeezed his eyes shut, then he turned to her, wrapping his arms around her shoulders and drawing her close. He held her tightly and buried his face in her hair. "I don't know what I'll do if I lose him."

She hugged him back, her hands pressing into the nylon of his ski jacket, her cheek snug against the front of his cotton shirt and the warmth of his chest. "You're not going to lose him," she managed through her tears. "He's a tough little guy. A real fighter."

"How could I do this to him?"

Kari leaned back to look at his face. She saw the guilt. "David, you're not the one to blame. You heard the paramedic. Only a small number of people are allergic to oysters."

"But I should have known. We're talking about my son."

"And how could you have known? I doubt Gail knew. She used to eat my mother's oyster dressing. Nothing ever happened to her. She could have been the one with Timmy today." And if she had been, Kari doubted Gail would have acted as swiftly or efficiently as David had.

"Great. So I'm the one he got the allergy from."

"Did you sample the dressing while you were making it?"

"Well . . . yes."

"And did you get sick?"

It was obvious he hadn't.

He sighed. "So why did Timmy?"

"Who knows? Recessive genes. Whatever. David, you're a wonderful father. You cared enough to come halfway across the country to find your son, and then when you did find him, as angry as you were with Gail, you thought about Timmy first, not your wants or your anger. You take time for him, listen to him. In the two months you've been here, I've seen changes in Timmy. Marvelous changes. He's gone from sullen and angry to happy and playful."

"And now he's in the hospital, fighting for his life." Again David closed his eyes, his shoulders sagging. "I feel so helpless."

So did she. How she wished she had the words to make everything right. "Don't forget, the fortune-teller saw three children in your future. She didn't say anything about you losing one."

He scoffed. "I thought you didn't believe in that fortune-teller."

At the moment, she was willing to believe in anything. "You never know."

David knew Kari was only trying to console him, that believing in fortune-tellers was as foolish as believing in magic. Still it was reassuring to remember that the fortune-teller hadn't mentioned death, only to beware of someone he trusted. It was also ironic that he was beginning to believe she was right about that. If he wasn't careful, even if Timmy lived, he might lose him. "Why do I keep screwing up my life, Kari?"

"Because life isn't easy. Because being a parent isn't easy. Just when you think you have all the answers, they change the questions. You're not screwing up any more than anyone else."

"I spent two and a half years in prison because of stupidity."

"You said yourself, you were framed."

"Framed because I refused to believe what I was seeing, because I blindly trusted others. I lost out on three years of my son's life, three years of his growing up. And now I may lose out on the rest of his life."

"He's going to make it," she said firmly.

He knew they were empty words. Neither of them knew if Timmy would make it or not. Softly, he blew into her hair. "Thank you for being here, for caring."

"How could I not care? Timmy's like family to me."

"He loves you, you know. He's told me he does, and you can see it in the way he acts with you. I've even heard him slip up sometimes and call you Mommy."

She looked up at him, and he could tell his words had bothered her. "I'm not trying to take him away from Gail," she insisted. "I just—"

"You're just a good little mommy."

"And he's—" She squeezed her eyes tight. "Oh, David—"

Kari buried her face against the front of his shirt and cried on a dozen levels. Some of her tears were for Timmy, some for David, and some for herself. Life had never seemed so precious, or so fleeting.

How could she go back to her house if Timmy didn't make it? How would she go on when the day came that he left? To look out her back window and not see him climbing his jungle gym or tossing corn to the ducks? To step into her bathroom and not remember him in the bathtub, splashing water all over the place—laughing and giggling? The bedroom he was using would always be his. His chair at the table . . . the stool he sat on at the counter.

He'd become a part of her, just as his little boy scent was a part of him, and his quick smiles and sullen pouts. She'd spent the past five years painting pictures for children. From now on, she would always be painting for Timmy.

"It's all right," David soothed, stroking her hair and rocking her in his embrace. "It's all right, honey."

She knew it would never be all right again. Telling Gail she'd watch Timmy had been a mistake. Opening that door to David had been a mistake.

She'd fallen in love with two men, one only four years old. Two men she would ultimately lose.

"Mr. Weeks?" a woman said from behind. "Mrs. Weeks?"

Kari turned toward the voice, wiping the tears from her cheeks and blinking her eyes clear. Standing in the doorway was a middle-aged woman in a white lab coat, a stethoscope around her neck. She smiled.

"I just wanted to let you know your son is out of danger. The epinephrine has taken effect, the hives are under control, and he's breathing normally again. We're moving him to a room right now. He'll need to stay here for a couple of days while we monitor his progress. We want to make sure there are no setbacks, but I don't think there will be any. Do you have any questions?"

"When can we see him?" David asked.

She smiled and glanced at her watch. "Give the nurses five minutes to get him ready. I'll have one come down and get you. You have a darling little boy."

"I know," David said and sighed in relief.

The moment the doctor left the room, he turned to Kari. "He's going to be all right. Timmy's going to be all right."

Her eyes glistened with tears and her grin covered her entire face. "I told you so."

The wind had mussed her hair and his tears had made it damp. What makeup she'd had on before dinner was long gone. Nevertheless, he'd never seen anyone more beautiful. Wrapping his arms around her, he squeezed her close. "Kari Carmichael, I love you."

"And I love you," she answered without hesitation.

He found her mouth and pressed his lips to hers. The tension drained from him, his relief complete. Life was good. People were good.

His son was alive.

David lifted his head for a moment and looked down at Kari. In her eyes he saw the same joy he held in his heart. He wanted to shout out his relief and turn cartwheels around the room.

What he did was kiss her again.

Boldly, he ravished her mouth, and she allowed him to, parting her lips and inviting him in. He accepted her invitation, pushing his tongue past her teeth to the moist warmth within. The groan he heard might have been from her or from him—he wasn't sure and didn't care. All he wanted was to touch and feel, to bury himself in her until all fears were forgotten.

Desire shot through him with unexpected force, rocking him back on his heels and taking his breath away. How little it took to stir the need—in him and in her. She could make her protests if she wanted, say it was wrong and they had no future, but she couldn't say the chemistry wasn't there, not if she were honest.

From the day he'd first met her, she'd changed his life. She'd taken his world of black and white and turned it to mediating grays, passionate pinks and sometimes the blues. As complex as her paintings, she was a collage of parts, sometimes the shy one, sometimes the fighter, and sometimes melting in his arms.

She was melting in his arms now, blending her kisses with his and pressing her body against his. How clearly he could remember the softness of her breasts, the feel of them. Even through her blouse and his shirt, he was aware of the tautness of her nipples, just as he was sure she was aware of his arousal. He wanted to tear away her clothing, to touch and kiss hers, to—

"Mr. and Mrs. Weeks?"

The hesitant voice broke through his haze of passion. Looking up, he saw a young nurse standing in the doorway. Her smile was knowing.

"You can see your son now."

"Thank you," he said hoarsely and looked down at Kari. She had her eyes closed and was breathing deeply. That she'd been affected as strongly as he had by their kisses pleased him.

They followed the nurse down the hall, saying nothing. Kari wasn't sure what to say. One kiss and her emotions were soaring. Two and her sanity had fled. He'd kissed her in relief and she'd been ready to give herself to him. Just because she'd meant her words of love didn't mean he had. She'd had a very good lesson about men while she was in college.

For two years Steve had said he loved her. She'd done his laundry, helped him with his projects and slept with him. And the day he graduated, he'd packed his bags. "What a man says in the throes of passion," he told her when she asked where he was going, "or in a moment of sheer relief, should never be taken too literally."

That was the last time she saw or heard from him. When Gail returned, David would also be gone.

The nurse slowed as they neared a door and turned toward them. "You're still going to see the hives. They'll take days, maybe weeks to completely go away. And he may seem a little jittery. That's the adrenaline in his system. He has an IV in his arm. He'll be getting steroids for a couple of days. Otherwise, he's looking pretty good for a guy so close to death."

Looking good, Kari decided, was a relative statement. That Timmy was alive was the best news anyone had given her, but seeing him in a hospital bed, plastic tubing running from his arm to an IV bottle hanging by his bed, she wanted to cry again. His eyes were still puffy and partially shut, and red blotches covered his exposed skin.

"Hi, Tiger," David said softy, going over to the side of Timmy's bed.

"Daddy?" Timmy managed a weak grin. "Did I really come here in a helicopter?"

"You really did. So did I."

"Neat-o. Wait till I tell Jason and Chad."

"You gave us quite a scare, guy." David took Timmy's unfettered hand in his. "How are you feeling?"

"Kinda funny." He looked around. Kari smiled when his gaze met hers.

He grinned back. "Hi, Mommy."

She didn't correct him. "Hi."

"Did you fly in a helicopter, too?"

"No, I had to drive the car."

"Where's Grandma and Grandpa Carm?"

"Back at the house." And she had to call them, let them know Timmy was all right.

"Did they get to fly in the helicopter?"

"No, just you and your daddy."

"Neat-o," he said again and looked up at his father. "You know what the doctor said? He said I peed like a racehorse when they gave me a shot. Isn't that silly."

Timmy giggled and David sighed, squeezing his son's hand. "Silly but true. Didn't know you had so much in you."

Again Timmy giggled, then yawned. Kari took that as a cue. "I'm going to go call my folks," she said, but before she left, she gave Timmy's toes a squeeze through the blanket. "Be back in a minute, mister."

As she walked out the door, she heard Timmy say, "Tell me about the helicopter, Daddy. Did we go way up high? Were you scared?"

Timmy came home on Saturday. He would be taking medication for the next week, and the hives weren't completely gone, but he was back to his old self, full of energy and always on the go.

It also snowed on Saturday. Big, fluffy flakes that clung to the tree branches, turning the landscape picture-postcard beautiful. "How I miss this," Liz Carmichael said, looking out Kari's kitchen window.

"Ready to move back?" Kari asked, letting the dish-water out of the sink.

Her mother chuckled. "No way, and neither is your father. Last year, every time we heard a weather report from back here, he'd say, 'Boy, am I glad I don't have to shovel that snow.' Sure you don't want to move down there? Another month from now you'll have a foot of snow on the ground and temperatures around zero."

"And next summer you'll have temperatures above one hundred."

"Everything's air-conditioned." Looking out the window, she laughed. "Your father just slipped trying to help Timmy and David build a snowman. He's got snow all over his rear end."

Kari walked over to look. The two men and Timmy were busy rolling balls of snow across the yard, a white patch across her father's rear. "Timmy likes him. He likes both of you."

"And we like Timmy... and David. If you're not going to take your father's advice and concentrate on advertising, we're glad to know you'll have David to help support you."

"He won't be supporting me," Kari said and knew she'd set herself up for another lecture. She also knew it was time to speak up. "I'm not giving up the illustrating, Mom. In fact, I'm going to submit an idea I have. It's called *When Daddy Comes Home*. I'll show you some sketches I've made."

She started to go get them, but her mother stopped her. "Honey, I know you like doing this, but your father's right. You're never going to make any money at it. Tell me, do you really like living in a dump like this?"

Kari looked around. She'd never thought of her house as a dump. It was old, yes, but she'd always felt its age gave the place character. And she did want better furnishings, but she'd always felt what she had was comfortable. David had called her place homey, and that's the way she liked it. Homey and comfortable.

"This house is certainly not what we'd pictured you living in," her mother said.

Closing her eyes, Kari tried to think of anything she'd ever done that had been what her parents had pictured. Even *she* wasn't what they'd pictured. They'd wanted a boy. She'd heard them tell that to others. And they'd wanted her to be a straight A student. She never was. They'd hoped for outgoing and gregarious. The closest she'd come to that was being friends with Gail, and they hadn't approved of her. Not one bit.

Her father had wanted her to go into business. Her mother had wanted her to marry money. On both counts, she'd let them down.

She heard David yell something to Timmy and knew if her parents were hoping for a union there, they were again going to be disappointed.

"Sometimes I just don't understand you," Liz Carmichael said.

Opening her eyes, Kari looked at her mother. "No, you don't."

"So are you going to marry him?"

"David?" She looked back out at him. "No."

"Why not?" Her mother was beginning to sound exasperated.

"Because once he gets custody of Timmy, he'll be moving back to California."

"And you wouldn't move?"

"He won't ask me."

"And what makes you so sure of that?"

"Little things." After what he'd said and the way he'd kissed her at the hospital, she'd had hope that they did have a future, but the few times they'd been alone since then, he'd acted distant and preoccupied. Almost as if he'd forgotten what had happened. Or wanted to forget it.

Considering what she'd found, she understood.

David had stayed with Timmy the rest of Thanksgiving Day, the next day and both nights. Kari had brought him his toothbrush and a change of clothes. Going through his drawers to find underwear and shirts had seemed an intimate act, but it was seeing the letter from Gail from Paris that had bothered her the most.

She didn't read it. She didn't need to. On the back of the envelope, Gail had put *x*s and *o*s. It was clear she had turned her eyes from her boss to David.

"What little things?" her mother persisted.

"I think he might get back together with Gail." Considering his attitude the first time she'd met him, the idea seemed incredible, yet the evidence was there. He'd sent Gail money. She was writing to him. Hardest for Kari to accept was the fact that it was for the best. "It would be great for Timmy if they did."

Kari's mother looked back out the window. Slowly, she shook her head. "I don't think so."

"If they fight over who's going to have custody of him, Timmy's the one who's going to be hurt," Kari argued.

"It might be best for Timmy, but that man is in love with you."

To hear her mother say it stunned Kari. "How do you know?"

Eyebrows raised, Liz Carmichael put an arm around Kari's shoulders and gave her a squeeze. "Because I—"

The telephone rang.

Her mother stopped what she was going to say and looked toward the phone. "That's probably Barbara. She said she might call this morning. We want to get together before your dad and I fly back."

Again the phone rang. Kari stepped away from her mother and answered it. The moment she heard the operator ask if she would accept the collect charges, she knew the call wasn't for her mother.

"Kari?" Gail asked. "How's Timmy?"

"Fine." She was surprised by the question. She hadn't called and told Gail what had happened to Timmy. David had said there was no need since Timmy was now doing fine and Gail would be back in another week.

"Is he home from the hospital yet?"

"Yes." Gail obviously knew. "David brought him home this morning."

"Is David there?"

"They're outside building a snowman."

"Could I talk to him? Please."

It was Gail at her sweetest, and Kari felt ill. "I'll get him," she answered and put down the phone.

Looking at her mother, she said, "Gail wants to talk to David." Then she went to the back door and called for him.

He came in with snow clinging to his hair and his cheeks a ruddy red. Stomping snow from his boots and pulling off his gloves and earmuffs, he shook his head, spattering droplets of melting snow across the linoleum. Kari watched him cross the kitchen to the phone, and knew she would never love another man as much as she loved him.

She waited until he'd said, "Hi, what's up?" When his tone softened and he said, "I told you not to worry," Kari left the room.

Chapter Eleven

Monday morning, David acted on his suspicions and called Peri Chemical. When he kept getting the answering machine, he grew more suspicious. If the sultry-voiced woman on the tape had said Peri employees were taking extra days off for the holiday, he might have bought into the idea, but her message that all sales personnel were either out of the office or busy didn't ring true, especially when, after calling on the hour every hour he kept getting the same message.

Tuesday, Kari and her parents were going to Grand Rapids to do some Christmas shopping. Kari had asked if they could take Timmy. David decided he would also tag along. That morning, he called in and asked for a personal business day.

Three hours later, he dropped off Kari, her parents and Timmy off at Woodland Mall and drove away in her van. He'd brought along with him a recent invoice from Peri Chemical and their bank's account transfer authorization form from the prior year. It didn't take him long to find

the street address printed at the top of the invoice, and he immediately understood why all payments went to a post office box. Peri Chemical was an empty warehouse with a For Sale sign on the front. The faint lettering on the building sign in no way spelled out Peri, and a glance through one of the windows was enough for him to know no one had occupied the offices for some time.

It took him longer to find the post office where he'd been mailing correspondence. "I'm concerned," he told the postal clerk who helped him. "They say they're not getting all of the letters I've mailed."

The postal clerk studied the address at the top of the invoice he'd showed her and frowned. "I don't understand why not," she said. "If you're addressing them to this box number and zip code, there should be no problems."

"This is the box for Peri Chemical?"

She nodded.

"Is there another name listed for this box?" he asked. "Someone authorized to pick up the mail?"

The clerk went through her files, finally pulling out an application form. "A Ms. Tanya Rice."

"No one else?"

"No one else." She smiled warmly. "Is there anything else I can do to help?"

The way she was looking at him, he was pretty sure she wasn't just talking about postal affairs. "Perhaps." He kept his smile just as warm. "Do you have an address for this Tanya Rice?"

For a moment, the clerk frowned, then a smile again crossed her face. Reading from the form in her hand, she gave him Tanya Rice's address.

Not that it helped. The address she gave him was for the same vacant warehouse David had just checked out. He'd gone in a full circle.

"Thank you very much," he said and left.

His next source was the bank with Peri Chemical's account. He knew he wouldn't be able to get much information from them, not without a court order, but he might be able to learn something. Stopping by, he asked to talk to the vice president in charge of electronic transfers. The man was friendly but evasive, and the only thing David learned was yes, all transfers from Bear Lake Resort had been properly credited to that account number.

More concerned than relieved, David slipped the invoice and transfer sheet back into the manila envelope. Tossing it into the back of the van, he drove to the mall. But before he went looking for Kari and the others, he stopped at a phone. It took him only a second to find a listing for T. Rice. A minute later, the same low, sultry voice from the Peri Chemical phone mail greeted him. "Is this Tanya Rice?" he asked.

Her yes was hesitant.

"You work for Peri Chemical?"

The immediate click and the sound of the dial tone surprised him. He was still staring at the receiver when he heard, "Daddy, guess who Aunt Kari took me to see?"

David tried not to think about what he'd learned while they had lunch. Timmy was talking a mile a minute, all of his energy and vitality back as he rambled on about his visit with Santa and what he wanted for Christmas. David hoped he'd be around for Christmas.

He didn't like the way things were shaping up.

That evening he willingly let Kari's mother read a bedtime story to Timmy. Sitting in Kari's living room, waiting for the time when he would say good-night to his son, David mulled over what to do next. Only when Kari sat down beside him did he drag his thoughts away from the problem.

She smiled, but he could tell the past few days were taking their toll. "For a woman who likes solitude, you cer-

tainly haven't been getting much lately," he said, giving her hand a squeeze.

Her father came into the room right then, and Kari merely squeezed David's hand back. How well he read her.

"I just finished talking to Jerry," her father said, seating himself in the chair across from them. "The fellow at that graphics shop in Phoenix that I told you about. He said if you decided to move to Arizona, you could have a job with them any time you wanted."

Kari knew the time had come to take a stand. Freeing her hand from David's, she sat straighter, took in a deep breath, then spoke. "Dad, I'm not moving to Arizona, and I'm not going into graphics, not as a career. I am a children's book illustrator. And hopefully, one day, I'll also be a children's book writer."

"But the money—" he began.

She cut him off. "Isn't that important to me."

His frown expressed his disbelief. "This would be steady income. And if you wanted to play around with your illustrating, you could still do it."

"Dad, I'm not *playing around* with my illustrating. It's what I love doing. Graphic work is fine, but it doesn't allow me the artistic freedom I have with my children's book illustrations. It doesn't give me the same satisfaction."

"Satisfaction is all well and good, but you need to think about your future. Your mother and I won't always be around to bail you out."

"When have I asked you to bail me out?" she returned, upset by the suggestion.

"Well, you know what I mean." He looked at David. "You tell her. Artistic freedom is a nice ideal, but in this world, money talks."

David rested a hand on hers. "I think she's doing exactly what she should be doing. What you need to do is listen to her."

Once again, her father frowned. "I see you have another one arguing for you."

"No, Dad, I don't need anyone arguing for me." And that was a good feeling. "I know what I want. It's not what you want, but it's who I am."

"Timmy said he's ready for his good-night kiss," Kari's mother said, stepping into the room. "In fact, if you don't hurry, he may already be asleep. That is one tired boy."

"I'll go to him," David said, rising from the couch.

Kari watched him leave the room, then she again faced her father. "I'm proud of you for what you're doing with your life, Dad. You started your own company, expanded it and moved it to where you've always wanted to live. But your goals aren't the same as mine. Maybe you'll never understand, but I hope someday you're proud of me."

"Honey," her mother said, coming over to sit beside her. "We're proud of you now. All we've ever wanted is for you to be happy."

Kari looked at her father, and he nodded. What surprised her most was she would have sworn he had tears in his eyes.

Thursday, Kari's parents left. She took Timmy with her when she drove them to the airport in Traverse City. On the drive back to Bear Lake, Timmy fell asleep and she found herself thinking. A few more days and Gail would be back and things would change. The battle for Timmy would really start . . . if there was a battle. Kari was no longer sure.

David had said Gail was calling him every day, just to talk. Kari knew what that meant. Gail was wooing David with words, with her lies, and he was sucking them up like a sponge. Not once in the past two weeks had he said anything bad about her. In fact, the one time Kari had grumbled about Gail, David had jumped to her defense.

Considering how distant he'd been lately, how lost in his thoughts he always seemed to be, she could read the writing on the wall. As usual, Gail was going to come up a winner. She would have her son and she would have David.

And Kari would be left with memories.

The moment David came over that evening, she knew there was a problem. He said little during dinner and barely touched his food. Timmy kept singing a song he'd heard on television. The fourth time he sang it, David snapped at him, then abruptly got up from the table. "I'm sorry," he said just as quickly, then looked at her. "Could you put him to bed tonight?"

He didn't give her a chance to answer. He walked away from the table and out of her house without once looking back.

"Daddy's not feeling well," Timmy said seriously. "I think he's got the fly."

"The fly?" she asked.

"Mrs. Van Housen said Jason and Cheryl had the fly. That's why they weren't at school yesterday. And Susan threw up after we had our juice. Mrs. Van Housen said she probably had the fly, too."

"Ah, the flu." Kari grinned, understanding. She was pretty sure David had something more serious than the flu.

She waited until Timmy was in bed and asleep before she donned her coat and boots and crossed the yard to Maude's house. When David didn't answer her knock on the side door, she let herself in. "David?" she called from the coatroom into the kitchen.

He stepped out of his bathroom, a towel to his face, and his white shirt unbuttoned and pulled from his trousers. Hanging open, it exposed his bare chest and she found her gaze following the hairs that trailed down to his belt buckle. That, too, was open.

"Timmy was afraid you might have the fly...I mean flu," she said quickly, looking back up at his face.

"What made him think that?" He walked toward her, but didn't button his shirt or buckle his belt.

She forced herself to focus on his eyes—those beautiful, blue eyes. "Uh—a couple of kids have it, I guess. And one little girl got sick in class."

"Meaning he'll probably get it too." David stopped directly in front of her. "Well, you can tell him I don't have the flu." He touched the side of her face, his gaze making her heart flip. "How are you doing? Sad to see your parents gone or glad?"

"A little of both," she said. "At least I feel we got a lot of things straightened out." But her relationship with her parents wasn't what she was worried about. "How about you, David? How are you doing?"

He shrugged and let his hand drop back to his side.

"What's up?"

"What do you mean, what's up?"

"I mean something's bothering you. It has been for some time now." She steeled herself and asked the question that had been gnawing at her all day. "Is it Gail? Are you worried about her coming back, about how you're going to feel?"

"No, it's not Gail." David wished it were that simple.

"Then what is it?"

He debated telling her, then decided she would learn sooner or later. Perhaps it would be better if he was the one to explain. "I think that fortune-teller was more on target than we gave her credit for."

Kari frowned. "Meaning?"

"Meaning once again someone I trusted has betrayed my trust. That I didn't learn my lesson the first time."

"Who betrayed your trust?"

"Wayne Peterson. Here I thought the man was behind me one hundred percent, thought I owed him for talking Wilkerson into giving me my job. Actually thought he was my friend." David hated to admit his stupidity. It was like déjà vu.

"I didn't suspect Wayne, not until just recently. When I first asked him about Peri Chemical, his explanation sounded perfectly feasible. Golf greens and swimming pools do need chemicals. Snow-making machines need chemicals. Starting out at a new job, there was so much for me to learn—the accounting system, how to run that damn computer. I didn't have time to check into individual accounts, not until just recently. It was last week, just before Thanksgiving, that I realized how much we'd spent in the past year on those chemicals. Still, it wasn't until Tuesday that I knew for sure that things weren't on the up-and-up."

"Tuesday?" she asked. "When you took a personal business day and went down to Grand Rapids with us?"

He nodded. "The Wednesday before Thanksgiving I was figuring up how much we'd paid Peri Chemical in the past six months, and it came to more than fifty thousand dollars. That seemed a hell of a lot of money for chemicals. Wayne wasn't around, so I called Peri Chemical. All I got was an answering machine, but since it was the day before a holiday, I didn't think too much of that. Lots of companies were closing down early, letting their employees off. I had Friday off. But Monday I tried again, and still all I got was an answering machine. Your decision to go down to Grand Rapids on Tuesday was perfect timing. It gave me a chance to visit Peri Chemical in person. And what I discovered is this chemical company that's supposedly been delivering thousands of dollars' worth of chemicals to Bear Lake Resort is nothing more than an empty warehouse, and the address I've been mailing letters to is a post office box that was rented by a woman. The same sultry-voiced woman who's on the answering machine."

"You never said anything Tuesday."

She sounded hurt. He'd hadn't known what to say. "Your folks were around. There wasn't exactly the opportunity."

"Last night?" she asked. "Tonight?"

"Kari, I didn't want to involve you. Beside, I thought I had everything under control. Now that I knew what was up, I was going to protect myself, collect as much data as I could and turn Wayne in. When I did tell you, I wanted it to be a fait accompli." He shook his head. "But that's not what's going to happen."

Kari heard the defeat in his voice and saw it in his eyes. Reaching out, she placed a hand on his sleeve, the tension in his body traveling up through her fingertips.

"Yesterday," he said, "I spent the entire day gathering evidence. Anything and everything I thought I might need—letters, invoices. I even made printouts of all the transactions that involved Peri Chemical. I was going to bring that stuff home with me, keep it here, then call Wilkerson and let him know what I suspected. But before I got a chance to take the file out to my car, Wayne came into my office. I've got to say, I admire the man. He asked what I was doing, and when I told him my suspicions, he acted as though he had no idea what was up. He looked through those papers as if the whole thing was just dawning on him, then he said we had to call Wilkerson."

David kept shaking his head. "I watched him dial the number and heard him talk to the man. At that point, I didn't know what to think, but when he told me to go ahead and take the file home with me, I thought I'd been wrong about him, that he was as much in the dark about Peri Chemical as I'd been. It wasn't until he was about to step out of my office that he said he remembered why he'd come by. Cool as a cucumber, he said Tom over at the pro shop needed to see me about an account. Wayne asked if I would check on it before I took off. I did."

"And the file?"

"I put it in my car. Locked my car. I know I did. What I'd forgotten was way back in early October Wayne had seen some keys in my desk drawer and had asked what they were for. I'd told him that ever since I'd locked my keys in the car, I'd always kept a spare set around. While I was over at the pro shop, he must have taken that set, gotten into my car and switched files on me because last night, after I left your place and came back here, I opened up that file and discovered what I had was a stack of incoming bills, none from Peri Chemical."

"All the evidence you'd collected was gone?"

"Everything. And today, Wayne Peterson was also gone. Out sick, his secretary said. Out visiting a Grand Rapids bank and one sultry-voiced woman, I'd say."

"So he's taken off, left you to take the rap?"

He chuckled. "You've been watching too many cop shows. But yes, that about sums it up."

"Well, just run another copy of what you have on your computer. That should be all the evidence you need."

"Sounds good . . . if there were any computer records to run copies of." He released a frustrated sigh. "They're gone, Kari. Remember I told you Wayne was a genius when it came to computers. Well, he is. I never truly appreciated how much of a genius. Anything and everything that involved Peri Chemical has been wiped out of my computer, out of all of the resort's computers. Peri Chemical no longer shows up on my balance sheets, on the accounts payable, on anything. It's as though this company never existed, which, of course, it didn't.

"That doesn't sound possible."

The moment she said it, she wished she hadn't. David pulled his arm away from her hand, his entire body stiffening. His tone, when he spoke, was sharp. "Well, believe it or not, it is possible. All of this is possible. But then, why should you believe me? No one believed me three and a half years ago when they arrested me for embezzling money from our investment firm. Not the police.

Not the jury. Not even Gail." He laughed, but without mirth. "She said, 'Just my luck to marry a dumb thief.'"

Kari flinched at the words, knowing his hurt. "David, I'm not the police, nor a jury, nor Gail. I may not understand how something can be done, but that doesn't mean I don't believe you. The question is, what do we do next?"

"We?" He shook his head. "No, I'm not getting you involved. I haven't even told you the worst."

There could be worse? "Which is?"

"I spent most of the morning trying to find those missing files. It wasn't until this afternoon that I started checking the balances in the files that remained. We're no longer talking about fifty thousand dollars having been paid to some Peri Chemical. Now my balance shows a quarter million dollars missing."

"And Wilkerson's coming?"

"If Wayne actually made that phone call. And I suspect he did. Now that I look back on it, all Wayne was doing was covering his butt, giving himself a little breathing room. Wilkerson's going to suspect me. He was suspicious of me when he first interviewed me. By the time someone realizes Wayne isn't home sick, he's going to be out of the country and I'm going to be left holding the bag. As I said, I've been here before. Only last time I didn't have any warning. I left my office on a Friday evening thinking everything was fine, and Monday morning, I returned to find my secretary crying and two police officers ready with the handcuffs."

"Well, to be forewarned is to be forearmed," Kari assured him, and headed for the telephone on the wall. "If those files have been deleted, I know just the man to get them back."

"And who might that be?" he asked, dumbfounded by her action.

"Ralph. Wayne Peterson might be a genius when it comes to computers, but he used to call Ralph for help. Ralph is a supergenius."

"And you think Ralph is going to help me?" David laughed, coming up behind her. "Honey, the man would be glad to see me hang."

She glanced back and grinned, then punched in seven numbers. "Maybe, but he also loves a challenge."

Kari paced the floor, waiting for David to return. Ralph had been predictably curious when she'd explained the problem. He'd also been predictably reluctant to do anything for David. "He's feeding you a bucket of bull," he'd said. "Don't you find it interesting that this is the second time this has happened to the man?"

"Absolutely fascinating," she'd answered sarcastically. "Will you help him or not?"

Ralph hadn't said anything for a minute, and she'd mentally kicked herself for letting her temper rule her judgment. Then he said, "I'll do it, but not for him. I don't want you involved in this in any way."

"He'll meet you at the resort in fifteen minutes," she'd told David after she hung up.

That was the second time David Weeks told her he loved her. It happened so quickly, she almost didn't hear the words. One swoop and she was in his arms, her feet lifted off the linoleum, her open coat and sweatshirt pressing against his bare chest as he said it. And then his mouth was on hers, his kiss smothering and wonderful, and over too quickly.

The next second, he'd turned away and was buttoning his shirt. Two minutes later, he was on his way out the door. "I'll let you know what happens," he'd said as he left, then he'd smiled. "Thanks."

David opened Kari's front door slowly, not wanting to make a sound. He'd seen her from outside, all curled up on the couch. The television was on, color images moving about on the screen, but he doubted she was watching. The way she was lying, he was pretty sure she was asleep.

He wouldn't have come over at all as late as it was if he hadn't promised her he would. Or maybe he would have. This might be the last time he'd have a chance to see her, to touch her.

As quietly as he could, he closed the door behind him. People leaving their doors unlocked was one thing he hadn't gotten used to and he wasn't convinced it was a good idea, even if Kari insisted she was perfectly safe. Looking at her, all snuggled up like a pretzel, he wasn't sure she was all that safe. The thoughts racing through his head weren't exactly saintly.

From the first time he'd seen her, he'd wanted to make love with her. Back then he'd blamed the feeling on rampant hormones. Now the reasons were more complex. He'd laughed with her and cried with her. They'd shared kisses that had taken them to the brink of ecstasy. It only seemed right that they should go all the way, that they should have one night together.

Was it too much to ask?

In the morning, the life he'd known here at Bear Lake would come to an end. Once again he would be separated from those he loved, denied the pleasure of watching his child grow into manhood. Once again, he would be thrown behind bars for being too trusting.

David crossed the room to the couch. Easing down on the end, he reached out and touched Kari's leg. Immediately her eyes snapped open.

Emotions sprinted across her face: first alarm, then recognition, then pleasure. "Hi," she said softly and unwound to a sitting position. "How'd it go?"

"Not good," he admitted. "He couldn't do it."

Chapter Twelve

"Ralph couldn't retrieve any of the files?" Kari asked, her mind still drugged with sleep. "What are you going to do, then?"

David shrugged and leaned back against her couch, closing his eyes. Jay Leno introduced a guest on the television, and Kari realized then how late it was and how tired David must be. Reaching over, she hit the red button on her remote and the television went silent, the entire room now dark.

"Ralph tried everything he knew?" she asked, hoping for some way to prove David innocent, some way to retrieve what Wayne Peterson had wiped out.

"He took my computer with him," David said, a distance to his voice. "He said he'd try something else tomorrow, but he didn't hold out much hope."

She felt David's hand tighten on her leg, his fingers squeezing her calf muscle. "I was wrong about him. You should marry him."

"I have no say in this matter?" That he was palming her off on Ralph irritated Kari.

"He really loves you."

"And what about you?" she asked. He'd said it twice.

She thought she heard him sigh. She wasn't sure. Then he moved his hand away from her leg, the absence of its warmth leaving her with a sense of desolation. "Forget I ever said those words to you. I shouldn't have."

She couldn't forget. "The question is, did you mean them?"

Her living room was deathly quiet, the only sound in the house the hum of the refrigerator, yet she barely heard his "no." Squeezing her eyes tight, she told herself he was lying, that he did love her. His next words changed her mind.

"I'm glad Gail's coming back tomorrow," he said and pushed himself up from the couch. "You don't need to pick her up. I will. There's certainly no sense in my going to work."

"Do you love her?"

"Kari, it doesn't matter. I have no future."

He hadn't answered her question.

"But do you love her?"

She heard him take in a deep breath and exhale it. His answer came like a knife in the darkness, swift and cutting. "Yes."

He moved away from the couch. She could tell when he bumped into the chair. The lump in her throat stopped her from saying anything. Not until he opened her front door did she remember the little boy sleeping in her bedroom. "Are you going to take Timmy with you when you pick up Gail?"

"No," he said without hesitation. "Gail and I are going to need some time to talk. Go ahead and take him to nursery school."

He left, but she didn't move. *Take Timmy to nursery school. Forget I said I loved you.* She could do the former but not the latter. Yet both times he'd said the words had been moments of great relief, not times when sanity or logic reigned. Should she hold him accountable for expressing a passing emotion? Was it his fault he didn't share what she felt for him?

"Damn you for ever coming to Michigan," she cursed into the darkness. "And damn you, Gail, for ever asking me to watch Timmy."

Kari rose from the couch and started for her bedroom. When she stepped on one of Timmy's blocks, she really began cursing. The words, however, didn't stop the tears.

She didn't see David in the morning. His car was gone when she got up. Every time Timmy heard a noise, he ran to the living room window, certain it was his father with his mother. Kari tried to explain it wasn't time, then finally gave up. Time only had meaning to those who felt it was running out.

When Timmy said he didn't want to go to nursery school, Kari didn't have the heart to force him. It would be the last few hours she had with him. "I'm going to miss you, you know," she said, trying to cuddle him on her lap.

He wiggled and twisted until he was standing in front of her. "I'm still going to come see you every day, Aunt Kari," he insisted. "What if the ducks come back? Who would feed them?"

"Well, I don't think those ducks are going to come back until it gets much warmer." She glanced out at the fine flakes of snow that had been falling for the past hour. "And that's going to be a while."

"Well . . ." He shrugged his shoulders, just as David always did, and Kari felt a prickling of tears in her eyes.

"Well," she parroted, shrugging her own shoulders and making herself grin.

"I'll come anyway," he said very solemnly. "Okay?"

"Okay," she agreed with a nod. "What do you say we make a welcome-home card for your mother. Think she'd like that?"

"Yeah." He was heading for her studio before she even got to her feet. The phone rang as she pulled out paper and crayons for Timmy. He ran back into the living room to draw his card. She stayed in her studio and answered the phone.

It was Ralph.

"David there?" he asked.

"No, he went to pick up Gail." Kari glanced at the clock by her easel. "They should be back in the next half hour."

"Tell him it didn't work."

She understood what he meant. The news was like a kick in the gut. "You couldn't get anything?"

"Nothing I can make any sense of. There's a guy in California who might be able to help me. I've asked him for help in the past and he's been able to come up with solutions I'd never thought of. I left a message on-line for him, but it's only eight out there. He rarely gets on before eleven Pacific time."

"So there's still a chance?"

"I wouldn't bank on it, honey." He paused, then said softly, "I'm sorry, Kari. Actually, he's not a bad guy."

"He said kind of the same thing about you." She sighed, remembering. "He said I should marry you."

"Well then, that's another thing we agree on. Want to set a date?"

"I don't think so." She smiled in spite of the heaviness in her heart. "I'm just one of those idiots who wants what she can't have."

"He's a lucky guy."

"If he were lucky, you'd find a way to bring those files back."

"I'll keep trying," Ralph assured her.

By the time she walked back into her living room, Timmy had two pieces of paper covered with figures. She noticed his drawings of people were becoming more complex, though the bodies were still potato-shaped and the legs never quite matched.

When she pointed to the one figure separated from the other three, he surprised her by his explanation. "That's Mommy. She's come to see us."

"Us being . . . ?"

He looked up at her, his eyes an innocent blue. "You and me and Daddy. We're a family."

"Actually, I'm not part of your family, Timmy," Kari said. "I'm just a good friend. Your family is your mommy, your daddy and you." She pointed at each figure, then to the space above. "Shall I write 'Welcome home' up here?"

"Okay." He watched her write the letters, his little brow furrowed, then he touched her arm. "You could be my mommy," he said seriously. "Jason has two mommies. One he lives with and one his daddy lives with. Daddy could live with you."

"Your daddy may not be able to live with any of us for a while," she started, then heard a car pull into the yard. So did Timmy. Running to the window, he looked out. Kari glanced at her watch. David had gotten back earlier than she'd expected.

"It's the police," Timmy said, his nose pressed up against the glass. "They've gone to Daddy's house."

Kari went over to look. It was a sheriff's patrol car, and another came down the drive, pulling in behind the first. She recognized the first deputy when he stepped out of his car. Middle-aged and potbellied, he was the same man who'd come to her rescue three months ago. The second deputy, however, was different. Guns drawn, the two headed for Maude's front door.

"I think your daddy just ran out of time," she said, and wished there was some way she could let David know what was awaiting his arrival.

"Are they going to shoot Daddy?" Timmy asked, worried.

"No," Kari answered, putting on her coat and boots. "But they're going to take him away for a while. You stay here."

She gave Timmy a kiss, then went outside to talk to the deputies. "David's in Traverse City, picking up his ex-wife at the airport," she told them.

The middle-aged deputy glanced at the second. "Get on the radio and give them a description over there. Maybe they can pick him up before he gets out of the country."

"He's not leaving the country," Kari insisted. "He's picking up his ex-wife."

The deputy holstered his gun and ambled her way. "And what makes you so sure of that?"

"His son's in my house, for one thing. He wouldn't leave the country without Timmy."

"Well, maybe a quarter of a million dollars has more of a pull than paternal ties."

"He didn't take that money," she insisted, shivering.

The deputy noticed. He nodded toward her house. "Let's go inside and talk."

"When David arrives, you're not going to do anything in front of Timmy, are you? Pull guns? Handcuff David? You guys scared him enough last time."

"You seemed pretty pleased to see us, last time," the deputy reminded her. "But then . . ." He glanced at the house next door. "I guess you two have gotten pretty chummy the past few months."

"We've become friends," she said and gave him an icy look. "David was framed. Wayne Peterson is the man you should be looking for. It's Peterson who's taken that money. He's made it look like David's the guilty one."

"That's what Weeks told you?"

She knew he didn't believe a word she'd said. The man saw her as a gullible girlfriend, too lovesick to know when she'd been duped by a slick embezzler.

"Hey, they've picked him up," the second deputy called over from his car. "He was heading south on 131."

Kari stared at the first deputy. South on I-131 meant David hadn't gone to the airport, hadn't picked up Gail. Maybe she had been duped.

No sooner did the thought cross her mind than she heard the engine of another car and saw the deputies look up her drive.

David understood what was happening the moment he turned down the drive. "Just like old times, isn't it?" he said to Gail. "Police cars to greet us. Me being hauled off to jail."

She looked his way. "I suppose this means no child support?"

"Always worried about the money, aren't you?" He parked the car. "If I beat this, Gail, I'm going for custody."

"Give me a good settlement and you've got it," she said and reached over to take his hand. "Believe it or not, I hope you do beat this."

As far as Kari was concerned, the next few minutes were a terrible nightmare. David got out of his car with his hands up. The second deputy shoved him against the hood, forced him spread-eagle and handcuffed him. Timmy came running out of the house, screaming for his daddy, and Kari grabbed him as he ran by. Holding him in her arms all the while he twisted and kicked, she tried to explain what was happening. Only she didn't know how to explain, not to a four-year-old and not to herself.

Gail didn't get out of the car until the deputy insisted she step out. Then she purred in her sweetest voice and batted her eyes, and in seconds had him convinced she knew nothing of what had happened. "I've been out of the country," she said dramatically. "And now I'm back for my baby."

She held out her arms for Timmy, but he refused to go to her. It was his father he was watching. His father being shoved into the sheriff's car.

Like an animal, Kari thought, closing her eyes to the scene. She could imagine how David felt. She could feel the pain herself.

And then it was over. The sheriff's cars were gone, David was gone, and Gail had settled herself down in at Kari's living room and was fussing over Timmy. "How you've grown," she said, holding out her arms. "Come give Mommy a big hug."

He shook his head and glared at her. "I want my daddy."

"Well, I didn't take him away." Gail glanced at Kari. "Tell him I didn't take him away."

"He knows," Kari said, disturbed by how quickly Timmy had slipped back into the role he'd played before Gail had left. "He's just upset. Timmy, your daddy will be back just as soon as he can. In a little while, I'll go pay some money so he can come home." At least she hoped she had enough money to make whatever bond they set. "Meanwhile, your mommy's missed you. Can't you give her a hug?"

Reluctantly, Timmy gave Gail a hug, then he ran out of the room and to his bedroom, slamming the door. Gail burst into tears. "I shouldn't have stayed away so long."

"No, you shouldn't have." Kari stared at her friend, not sure how real Gail's tears were. "You should have come back the day David showed up. Should have been here for both of them. Damn it, Gail, aren't you worried about David?"

The tears did end, and Gail wiped her cheeks. "He's a big boy. He got himself into this mess. Why should I worry?"

"He loves you."

"David?" Gail looked up and laughed. "Once, yes…maybe. But even then, he didn't love *me,* not the me you know. He fell in love with an image I created for him."

"He said he understands you better now."

"Then he's one up on me. I still don't understand myself."

"So you don't love him?"

"No." Gail shook her head. "I loved the man I wanted him to be—the rich, successful businessman. I was looking for a man able to give me everything I wanted, everything I ever dreamed of as a child. I'm still looking for that man. For a while there, I thought it might be Vernon. What a disappointment that was." She sighed, then grinned. "But I did get to spend the fall in Paris, buy lots of clothes and go skiing in the Alps. It wasn't all bad."

"What about Timmy?" Kari asked. "While you were spending your fall in Paris and skiing in the Alps, he was here, living with a virtual stranger. You can't just dump him on someone every time you meet a man you think might fit your image."

"David said he wants custody of Timmy if he isn't sent to prison." Again, she sighed. "This really is a bummer."

"And you'd give Timmy to David?"

Gail looked at her. "He'd be a good father, wouldn't he?"

"A great father."

"Yeah." Gail nodded. "If he weren't facing ten to twenty years in prison."

Which did present a problem.

Timmy's door opened and he poked his head out. "Aunt Kari, I can't find my purple dinosaur."

"Where did you last see him?" she asked, trying to remember herself.

"In the van?"

She wasn't sure. "I'll look." Excuse me a minute, she told Gail. "Time to look for your dinosaur."

"What I need is a cup of coffee." Gail glanced over at Timmy. "You have any idea where your Aunt Kari keeps the coffee?"

Timmy came out of his room to show his mother, and Kari slipped on her coat and boots. Outside she shivered in the cold. The snow had nearly filled the sheriff's cars' tire tracks and was piling on top of David's car and her van. A sprinkling fell on her hands when she slid open the back door and climbed into the van. "Here, Barney," she called out, knowing fully well the stuffed dinosaur wouldn't answer. "Where'd you hide?"

Five minutes later she stepped back into the warmth of her house, Timmy's dinosaur in one hand and a manila envelope in the other.

Don Wilkerson was a tall, energetic man in his late forties. Kari liked the way he listened when she explained what the invoice and bank transfer printout she'd dumped out of the manila envelope onto his desk meant. She also liked the way he didn't waste time. A punch of a button and he had his secretary calling the bank in Grand Rapids. Two minutes later, he was talking to the bank manager.

Kari couldn't hear what answers Wilkerson got to his questions, but his expression told her he didn't like those answers. When he hung up the phone, he leaned back in his chair and looked at her. "Bear Lake Resort made a transfer of two hundred thousand dollars to the Peri Chemical account sometime between Wednesday night and Thursday morning. The money was withdrawn Thursday afternoon by a man fitting Wayne Peterson's description. He had a young woman with him. A sultry-voiced woman, according to the manager's description. Sounds like the one you were telling me about.''

''So they got away with it?'' Kari asked.

''Until we catch them.'' He smiled. ''I'm from Chicago, remember. I have friends who know how to deal with situations like this. They won't get far.''

''And David?'' She wasn't sure he believed David had nothing to do with the scheme.

''He should have called me the moment he suspected something was up.''

''Under the circumstances,'' she said, ''he wanted evidence first.''

Wilkerson nodded. ''I understand. These two pieces will help when Peterson decides to turn himself in.'' Again he smiled. ''Which he will. But more would have been nice.''

As if on cue, a secretary came to the door. ''There's a call for Ms. Carmichael,'' she said. Wilkerson motioned for her to pick up the phone.

''Yes?'' Kari asked cautiously.

''Gail said you'd be here,'' Ralph said on the other end. ''I did it. They're back. All of them.''

''The files on Peri Chemical?'' She looked at Wilkerson.

''All of them,'' Ralph repeated, and she mouthed the words to Wilkerson. He gave her the okay sign, and she sighed. ''Thank you, Ralph. I love you.''

''How I wish.'' He chuckled. ''He's a good man, Kari. Invite me to the wedding.''

''As I said,'' Kari repeated after hanging up the phone. ''About David?''

Wilkerson buzzed his secretary again. ''Get the sheriff's office for me.'' Waiting, he looked up. ''If you're going to pick him up, you'd better get going. Tell him to take the rest of the day off, but I want to see him tomorrow morning.''

''And when you see him?''

Wilkerson grinned. ''Think he might be interested in the position of manager?''

David wasn't sure what miracles Kari had worked, he only knew it felt good to walk out of the sheriff's office a free man. ''Okay, give,'' he said the moment they were seated in her van.

She smiled and started the engine. On the way to her house, she explained, starting with the envelope she found when she was looking for Timmy's dinosaur and ending with Wilkerson's offer. ''You've got a job, if you want it.'' She parked in front of her house and faced him. ''But I imagine you'll be heading back to California.''

''Not without Timmy.''

''I think Gail will let you have him. It might take a little while for the two of you to get everything legal, but she more or less told me she'd give you custody. And maybe, during that time, you can get her to fall in love with you again.''

He reached over and took her gloved hand in his. ''And why would I want to do that?''

Her gaze dropped to where his glove covered hers, then snapped back up to his face. ''You said you loved her.''

He could see the hope in her eyes and couldn't stop himself from grinning. ''I guess I've learned how to lie from the two of you.''

''I don't lie.''

''That's right, you don't.'' His grin disappeared. ''They say if you hate someone, you still have feelings for that person. When I arrived here, I hated Gail. Or, at least, I thought I did. I hated her for not standing by me, for divorcing me and for not being there when I was freed. I hated her for all the lies and for taking my son from me. Now—''

He gazed into Kari's doe-soft eyes and forgot the bitterness and anger. ''Now?'' she reminded him.

Again, he smiled, his tone softening. ''Now it doesn't matter. Now I've found someone who will stand by me, who doesn't lie and who has brought me closer to my son. Thank you for being there, Kari. I do love you, you know.''

''I kinda hoped so.''

He saw the tears in her eyes, each a liquidy gem he would always treasure. ''And do you love me?''

''With all my heart and soul.''

He leaned toward her, and she met him halfway, their lips touching in duo. He had a feeling it would always be like that, their kisses and their lives a shared experience, neither in control, each receiving as much as was given. Each a part of the other.

Remembering one thing, David sat back. ''Timmy's part of the package.''

She laughed. ''Timmy and another boy and a girl. Don't forget the fortune-teller. She's been right on so far.''

''Three children.'' He considered the number. ''I guess I'd better take that job as manager, and hire Gail as my secretary so we complete the prophecy. And we'd better find a bigger house.''

''That would please my folks. You're going to stay here then?''

He looked out the van's windows, the snow turning the landscape a fairy-tale white. It was a far cry from the sun and beaches of California. A far cry from the congestion and pollution, the gangs and the crime. Here you didn't lock your doors. It was just the place to raise a family. ''I'm going to stay. Maybe my folks can come out for Christmas.''

* * *

Gail and Timmy stood at the living room window looking out. "He's kissing her again." Timmy wrinkled his nose, then looked up at Gail. "Is she going to be my second mommy?"

"Looks like it," Gail said, then reached for his hand. "Come on, let's give them some privacy. I'll show you a key chain I got in Paris. It's shaped like the Eiffel Tower."

Epilogue

"My son absolutely loves *When Daddy Comes Home*," the woman on the opposite side of the table said. "That's why I'm getting a copy for my nephew. Could you make it 'To Peter'?"

Kari autographed the copy of the book in front of her "To Peter," then looked up. "What's your son's name."

"Alan." The woman leaned closer to see what she was doing. "We also have *Trolls, Fairies and Tommy Magoo*. Do you have anything new coming out?"

Kari wrote, "I hope you enjoy as much as Alan did" and signed her name, then looked up. "*Waiting for Daddy* should be on the stands just before Christmas. It's about a little boy and a little girl and what they do and the mischief they get into while they're waiting for their father to come home."

It was then that she noticed David coming through the mall toward the bookstore. Timmy was by his side, skipping and grinning, showing off his missing front teeth, and in David's arms was a little girl.

"You done yet?" Timmy asked, running ahead the last few feet.

"Mama," the little girl cried, twisting in David's arms and reaching out for Kari.

Kari took her daughter, giving her a kiss, then ruffled Timmy's hair, acknowledging him. "This is my family," she said, introducing them to the woman who still stood by the table. "My husband David, my stepson, Timothy, and our daughter, Caroline."

The woman looked at David and Timmy and smiled. "I know where you get your models."

"They do give me ideas," Kari said and tried not to smile when David lifted his eyebrows suggestively.

"I was her first model," Timmy said, pointing at the picture of the boy on the cover of *When Daddy Comes Home.* "And Caroline and I are in her next book. And when our brother arrives, he'll be in that book."

The woman looked at Kari's flat belly. "You already know you're going to have another boy?"

"We're pretty sure," David answered, moving closer and giving Kari a quick kiss on the cheek. "I brought the kids a little early. Hope you don't mind. Ralph suggested I get the latest issue of 'Compute.' Oh, and this came in the mail." He pulled a letter from his pocket. The handwriting was Gail's. "She's in Toronto. She got a small part in a TV series. She says it's her chance of a lifetime."

Kari grinned. "Now where have I heard that before?"

*　*　*　*　*

Silhouette

ROMANCE™

COMING NEXT MONTH

Conveniently Wed: Six wonderful stories about couples who say "I do"—and *then* fall in love!

#1162 DADDY DOWN THE AISLE—Donna Clayton
Fabulous Fathers
Jonas's young nephew was certainly a challenge for this new father figure. But an even bigger challenge was the lovely woman helping with the little tyke—the woman who had become this daddy's wife in name only.

#1163 FOR BETTER, FOR BABY—Sandra Steffen
Bundles of Joy
A night of passion with an irresistible bachelor left Kimberly expecting nothing—except a baby! The dad-to-be proposed a *convenient* marriage, but a marriage of love was better for baby—and Mom!

#1164 MAKE-BELIEVE BRIDE—Alaina Hawthorne
Amber was sure the man she loved didn't even know she existed—until the handsome executive made a startling proposal, to be his make-believe bride!

#1165 TEMPORARY HUSBAND—Val Whisenand
Wade's pretty ex-wife had amnesia—and forgot they were divorced! It was up to *him* to refresh her memory—but did he really want to?

#1166 UNDERCOVER HONEYMOON—Laura Anthony
Pretending to be Mrs. "Nick" Nickerson was just part of Michelle's undercover assignment at the Triple Fork ranch. But could she keep her "wifely" feelings for her handsome "husband" undercover, too?

#1167 THE MARRIAGE CONTRACT—Cathy Forsythe
Darci would marry—temporarily—if it meant keeping her family business. But living with her sexy cowboy of a groom made Darci wish their marriage contract was forever binding....

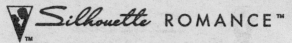

Silhouette ROMANCE™

is proud to present Elizabeth August's
TWENTY-FIFTH book—and the next installment
of her much-loved series:

Smytheshire, Massachusetts

This sleepy little town has some big secrets!

A HANDY MAN TO HAVE AROUND
by
ELIZABETH AUGUST
(SR#1157, June)

Gillian Hudson was determined to stay in Smytheshire, even
if it meant having Taggart Devereaux as her protector! But
this rugged loner never left her side, and Gillian suspected that
Taggart's "visions" weren't all about danger—but reflected her
own dreams of wedded bliss.

Don't miss **A HANDY MAN TO HAVE AROUND**
by Elizabeth August, available in June, only from

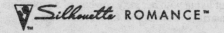

Silhouette ROMANCE™

EASMYTH

This July, watch for the delivery of...

An exciting new miniseries that appears in a different Silhouette series each month. It's about love, marriage—and Daddy's unexpected need for a baby carriage!

Daddy Knows Last unites five of your favorite authors as they weave five connected stories about baby fever in New Hope, Texas.

- **THE BABY NOTION** by Dixie Browning
  (SD#1011, 7/96)

- **BABY IN A BASKET** by Helen R. Myers
  (SR#1169, 8/96)

- **MARRIED...WITH TWINS!**
  by Jennifer Mikels
  (SSE#1054, 9/96)

- **HOW TO HOOK A HUSBAND (AND A BABY)**
  by Carolyn Zane
  (YT#29, 10/96)

- **DISCOVERED: DADDY** by Marilyn Pappano
  (IM#746, 11/96)

Daddy Knows Last arrives in July...only from

DKLT

SILHOUETTE... Where Passion Lives

Add these Silhouette favorites to your collection today!
Now you can receive a discount by ordering two or more titles!

SD#05819	WILD MIDNIGHT by Ann Major	$2.99	☐
SD#05878	THE UNFORGIVING BRIDE	$2.99 u.s.	☐
	by Joan Johnston	$3.50 can.	☐
IM#07568	MIRANDA'S VIKING by Maggie Shayne	$3.50	☐
SSE#09896	SWEETBRIAR SUMMIT	$3.50 u.s.	☐
	by Christine Rimmer	$3.99 can.	☐
SSE#09944	A ROSE AND A WEDDING VOW	$3.75 u.s.	☐
	by Andrea Edwards	$4.25 can.	☐
SR#19002	A FATHER'S PROMISE	$2.75	☐
	by Helen R. Myers		

(limited quantities available on certain titles)

TOTAL AMOUNT	$_____
DEDUCT: 10% DISCOUNT FOR 2+ BOOKS	$_____
POSTAGE & HANDLING	$_____
($1.00 for one book, 50¢ for each additional)	
APPLICABLE TAXES**	$_____
TOTAL PAYABLE	$_____
(check or money order—please do not send cash)	

To order, send the completed form with your name, address, zip or postal code, along with a check or money order for the total above, payable to Silhouette Books, to: **In the U.S.:** 3010 Walden Avenue, P.O. Box 9077, Buffalo, NY 14269-9077; **In Canada:** P.O. Box 636, Fort Erie, Ontario, L2A 5X3.

Name:_____

Address:_____City:_____

State/Prov.:_____ Zip/Postal Code:_____

**New York residents remit applicable sales taxes.
Canadian residents remit applicable GST and provincial taxes.

Silhouette®
™

SBACK-JA2

Conveniently Wed

"I do," the bride and groom said...without love
they wed—or so they thought!

#1162 Daddy Down the Aisle
Fabulous Fathers
Donna Clayton

#1163 For Better, For Baby
Bundles of Joy
Sandra Steffen

#1164 Make-Believe Bride
Alaina Hawthorne

#1165 Temporary Husband
Val Whisenand

#1166 Undercover Honeymoon
Laura Anthony

#1167 The Marriage Contract
Debut Author
Cathy Forsythe

Don't miss these six irresistible novels about tying the
knot—and *then* falling in love!

Coming in July, only from

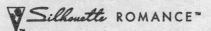 ROMANCE™

SOMETIMES BIG SURPRISES
COME IN SMALL PACKAGES!

Bundles of JOY

FOR BETTER, FOR BABY
by
SANDRA STEFFEN
(SR #1163)

A night of passion turned into an unexpected pregnancy for
Kimberly Wilson! So when Cort Sutherland learned he was a
daddy-to-be, he insisted on a convenient marriage. But with
vows exchanged, Cort and Kimberly realized they were still
almost perfect strangers! Could they live—and *love*—as
husband and wife before their bundle of joy arrived?

Conveniently Wed

"I do," the bride and groom said...without
love they wed—or so they thought!

Don't miss FOR BETTER, FOR BABY by Sandra Steffen, part of
the Conveniently Wed promotion, coming in July, only from

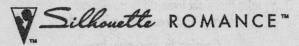
Silhouette ROMANCE™

BOJ796